W9-DIB-612

SWEPT AWAY

When Geoffrey's lips met hers, they softened and melded, drinking in the tart taste of lemons and the sweetness of Cassie Hartwell.

The kiss became more urgent. Geoffrey could hear Cassie murmur in the back of her throat, and the sound set him aflame. He slid his hands to her hips and was about to deepen the kiss when her gasp recalled him to where he was and what he was doing.

With an effort that was almost beyond him, Geoffrey moved his hands to Cassie's shoulders and set her away from him. He leaned his forehead against hers and, in a hoarse whisper, asked her forgiveness.

"Never." Cassie's voice was as unsteady as his.

Livonia Public Library
CARL SANDBURG BRANCH #21
30100 W. 7 Mile Road
Livonia, Mich. 48152
248-893-4010

BOOK YOUR PLACE ON OUR WEBSITE AND MAKE THE READING CONNECTION!

We've created a customized website just for our very special readers, where you can get the inside scoop on everything that's going on with Zebra, Pinnacle and Kensington books.

When you come online, you'll have the exciting opportunity to:

- View covers of upcoming books

- Read sample chapters

- Learn about our future publishing schedule (listed by publication month *and author*)

- Find out when your favorite authors will be visiting a city near you

- Search for and order backlist books from our online catalog

- Check out author bios and background information

- Send e-mail to your favorite authors

- Meet the Kensington staff online

- Join us in weekly chats with authors, readers and other guests

- Get writing guidelines

- AND MUCH MORE!

Visit our website at
http://www.kensingtonbooks.com

Just Say Yes

Myretta Robens

ZEBRA BOOKS
Kensington Publishing Corp.
www.kensingtonbooks.com

ZEBRA BOOKS are published by

NOV 0 4 2005

Kensington Publishing Corp.
850 Third Avenue
New York, NY 10022

Copyright © 2005 by Myretta Robens

All rights reserved. No part of this book may be reproduced
in any form or by any means without the prior written consent of the Publisher, excepting brief quotes used in reviews.

If you purchased this book without a cover you should be aware
that this book is stolen property. It was reported as "unsold and
destroyed" to the Publisher and neither the Author nor the Publisher has received any payment for this "stripped book."

All Kensington titles, imprints, and distributed lines are available at special quantity discounts for bulk purchases for sales
promotion, premiums, fund-raising, educational, or institu-
tional use.

Special book excerpts or customized printings can also be created to fit specific needs. For details, write or phone the office
of the Kensington Special Sales Manager: Attn. Special Sales
Department. Kensington Publishing Corp., 850 Third Avenue,
New York, NY 10022. Phone: 1-800-221-2647.

Zebra and the Z logo Reg. U.S. Pat. & TM Off.

ISBN 0-8217-7851-X

First Printing: August 2005
10 9 8 7 6 5 4 3 2 1

Printed in the United States of America

Livonia Public Library
CARL SANDBURG BRANCH #2
30100 W. 7 Mile Road
Livonia, Mich. 48152
248-893-4010

Chapter 1

"Kindly get your dog off me." Geoffrey Dorrington lay flat on his back in an unplowed field gazing up at the clear blue Devonshire sky while his face was thoroughly scoured by the rough tongue of a large canine. A canine that had obviously had fish for breakfast.

At the sound of a giggle, he squinted past the gray-brown fur of his assailant. The girl stood with both hands over her mouth, her eyes dancing in unalloyed merriment.

"I am gratified that my predicament amuses you—urgh." Geoffrey clamped his lips shut against further canine incursions.

"He is not my dog," the girl said, barely suppressed laughter infusing her voice. Nevertheless, she leaned over and, taking the huge beast by the scruff of his neck, pulled him off Geoffrey.

"Behave yourself, Brummell," she told the dog, pushing him onto his haunches and shaking a finger at him.

Geoffrey hauled himself to his feet and drew a sleeve across his face. "Brummell? That is the least likely Brummell I have ever seen."

"Well, he really has no name. At least as far as I

know. But I call him Brummell." She laid an affectionate hand on the dog's head.

"I thought you said he was not your dog." Glaring at the girl, Geoffrey ran his hands through his hair, and then began picking grass out of his clothing.

"Oh, he is not. He belongs to Mr. Jenkins, one of Bradworth's farmers. But he likes to follow me. Don't you, old fellow?" She looked fondly down at the dog.

"If he is part of your cohort, you might try to control him, my girl. He should not be allowed to run wild, attacking unsuspecting passersby." His improvised grooming completed, Geoffrey rested his fists on his hips and stared at the child.

And stared some more. This was no child. She could not have been many inches over five feet, her hair was a mass of curls around her face, and her wide green eyes had the ingenuous look of a young girl, but her drab brown dress covered curves where no child would have them. "Who are you?" he demanded.

"Sir?" The woman—for woman she obviously was—snapped her head up and stared at him. "I apologize, sir, for Brummell's . . . um . . . attack, but I'm sure he didn't hurt you. I really don't think that it's necessary to have my name. And," she added, "I might inquire the same. Who are you and what business do you have crossing this field?"

"Is this your field?" Geoffrey asked, trying not to grin at the girl's prim indignation.

She shook her head. "No."

Geoffrey cocked an assessing eyebrow at the impudent young woman. "Then perhaps you would not mind telling me why *you* are crossing it."

"I cross this field every day," she said, her eyes narrowed and her hands clenched. "My father is vicar of this parish, and I frequently visit the Bradworth tenants. I am sure the new owner will not object."

"Really? Well, that remains to be seen," Geoffrey said.

"You . . . you are not the new landlord?" For the first time in this bizarre conversation, the girl looked uncertain. Her eyes widened and her fingers curled into the hair on the huge dog's neck. The dog let out a low growl.

Geoffrey shot a quick, nervous glance at the dog.

"Hush, Brummell." The girl relaxed her hand, and the dog subsided. But she stayed quite rigid, watching Geoffrey with those huge green eyes.

"I am not," Geoffrey said and watched the girl—the vicar's daughter—relax her posture.

"I am, however, his new land steward, Geoffrey Dorton." Geoffrey bowed. "Your servant, Miss . . . ?"

The girl sighed. "I suppose you are bound to find out anyway," she said. "Miss Hartwell." She dropped a short curtsey, during which the wolfhound eyed Geoffrey speculatively.

"Very gracious," Geoffrey murmured.

"I must be going." Miss Hartwell shook her brown curls, twitched the skirt of her brown dress, put her hand on the back of the big brown dog, and turned away.

"Wait!" For a reason he could not name, Geoffrey was not ready to terminate the interview. Perhaps it was because she was the first person he had met outside of the workers on the Bradworth estate. Yes. Of course, that must be it. It was important to get to know the rest of the community.

Miss Hartwell stopped short but did not turn. "Yes?" she asked over her shoulder.

"I . . . er . . . mean to call on your father anyway. And, well, you seem to know the shortest route."

"Yes," she said.

"Would you mind if I accompanied you?" Geoffrey asked, chagrined to be begging the vicar's daughter for her company.

Miss Hartwell nodded and waited until Geoffrey stepped to her side—the side away from the dog.

"He won't bite," she said.

"He smells like a fish." Geoffrey raised his head, seeking the vibrant smell of Devonshire in the spring.

"And you smell like him," Miss Hartwell informed him, "so I would not be too quick to criticize."

"I do?" Geoffrey raised his arm and sniffed the sleeve of his jacket. "Oh Lord. I do. Perhaps I will call on your father another time."

"Oh, come along. We will keep Brummell between you and Papa and he will never notice." Miss Hartwell strode off and Geoffrey, sighing deeply, strode after her.

The Oakleigh vicarage looked surprisingly modern. The brick house had two sets of windows facing the road on either side of a well-proportioned entrance.

Geoffrey glanced down at his soiled and rumpled jacket and wondered if it was too late to excuse himself and come back when he was cleaner and neater and smelled better. Somewhere between the fallow Bradworth field and the main road in Oakleigh, Brummell had taken a different path, leaving Geoffrey the only one smelling like a fishy dog.

Miss Hartwell opened the front door and called into the house. "Mama, Papa, we have a visitor."

It was too late to leave. Straightening his jacket, Geoffrey stepped over the threshold.

The afternoon light streamed through the windows and revealed that the interior was not nearly as elegant as the outside. The rooms were small and the beams exposed. A musty smell pervaded the entry and Geoffrey was ridiculously glad that it would probably disguise his own questionable odor.

The kitchen opened up to the right of the entrance and a sitting room to the left. There was a staircase straight ahead, down which tramped three boys who looked to be eleven or twelve years old.

The boys were of varying complexions and sizes. He glanced at Miss Hartwell out of the corner of his eye. None of them looked like her. Were these her brothers?

"Miss Cassie, you're home. Capital," the largest boy called out as the third hit the last step. "We need help with our sums."

Ah, so Miss Hartwell was a Cassie. It fit her. But these couldn't be her brothers.

"Miss Cassie?" he asked.

"My name." The answer was curt. "Where is my father?" she asked the boys.

"In the garden, reading." The boys trooped into the kitchen, giving Geoffrey a quizzical glance as they passed him.

Geoffrey gave Miss Hartwell his own quizzical glance.

"Our boarders," she said. "My father's students."

"Ah." Not all that unusual for a country vicar to supplement his income by taking in students. And the vicarage looked to be large enough to accommodate the three boys and probably more.

Mr. Hartwell was in the back garden, sitting on a bench under an ancient apple tree. The creamy buds were just opening and the sweet perfume of apple blossoms enveloped Geoffrey as he followed "Miss Cassie" out the door.

Miss Hartwell marched purposefully across the lawn without waiting for Geoffrey, who hung back to observe the swaying of her skirts against her lovely, rounded bottom. How had he ever thought her a child? Every step wrapped the dun-colored gown around her legs. She might be short, but she was shapely.

". . . Dorton."

Geoffrey was startled by the sound of his assumed name. He had apparently been introduced to Miss Hartwell's father while he was busy admiring her bottom. He hoped the vicar had not noticed his unseemly inspection.

The vicar beamed as he rose and extended his hand. The top of his head came just to Geoffrey's chin and his eyes held a twinkle that was beginning to seem familiar to Geoffrey. "Dorton? New to Oakleigh, young man?"

"Yes, sir." Geoffrey shook the proffered hand. "I am here to see to Lord Marchbourn's estate."

"Marchbourn? Oh yes. Bradworth's heir. I was surprised to know there was an heir. Thought the place would revert to the crown. But we are pleased to have a new landlord. Does he mean to reside here?"

"I think not." Geoffrey shook his head. "I believe Lord Marchbourn means to stay in Somersetshire. He grew up there, you know, and is fond of the land. But I'm sure he'll be out to meet his new tenants once the planting is done at Marchbourn. He is a man who takes his obligations seriously."

"Naturally, naturally." The vicar smiled vaguely and looked longingly at the book in his hand. "But we are pleased he has sent a representative. I trust we shall see you again."

Geoffrey could tell he had been dismissed and was about take his leave of Miss Hartwell when a shrill voice sounded from behind a yew hedge at the back of the garden.

"Cassie, are you returned? Come over here right away."

Miss Hartwell flushed. "We have a guest, Mama," she said, a shade of annoyance in her voice.

A tall, spare figure emerged from behind the hedge, stripping off an apron and unceremoniously tossing it behind a shrub. Adjusting her cap, Mrs. Hartwell descended on the group beneath the apple tree.

"Well," she said, coming to rest directly in front of Geoffrey. "Who have we here?"

"This is Mr. Dorton, Mama. He is the new steward at Bradworth Hall."

Mrs. Hartwell looked Geoffrey up and down without once changing her expression. Her lean figure and angular features could not have been less like her daughter's. Cassie Hartwell obviously took after her father. Finally, the woman nodded. "Welcome to Oakleigh, Mr.—what did you say his name was?" She cut herself off in the midst of her greeting and turned to her daughter.

"His name is Mr. Dorton, Mama. I met him crossing the field near Mr. Jenkins's farm."

"And you spoke to him without an introduction?" By now, Mrs. Hartwell seemed to have completely forgotten Geoffrey's existence and had turned her full attention on her daughter.

Said daughter, despite being several inches shorter than her imposing mother, stood her ground. "Brummell had him pinned to the ground. I could not very well leave him in the middle of a field being licked to death."

"Brummell!" Mrs. Hartwell sniffed. "That dog is not your responsibility, nor is he called Brummell.

How many times must we discuss this unfortunate penchant of yours?"

"Mother." Miss Hartwell's posture had become ramrod straight, her chin was in the air, and her halo of brown curls fairly trembled with indignation. "We have a guest."

As the vicar, thoroughly absorbed in his book, did not even seem to notice the argument occurring in front of him, Geoffrey considered slipping away during Mrs. Hartwell's diatribe. Unfortunately he had not made up his mind before Miss Hartwell returned her mother's attention to him.

The vicar's wife turned slowly toward Geoffrey and resumed her critical inspection, almost as if she had not been interrupted. "New steward. Did you know the late owner?"

"No, madam," Geoffrey said, biting the inside of his cheek in an attempt to remain civil. "I was engaged by Lord Marchbourn."

"Hmmm. Don't know him." Mrs. Hartwell continued her inspection. "You look like you could use a bath."

"Madam?" Geoffrey took a quick step back, aware once again of his soiled jacket and his doggy odor and thoroughly startled that Mrs. Hartwell would indulge in such a personal observation.

"Mama." Miss Hartwell's musical voice was a welcome interruption. "Mama, Mr. Dorton's condition is not his fault. Perhaps you should invite him to supper at a time when he has not been trampled by a dog."

Mrs. Hartwell sniffed again, wrinkling her nose. "Supper? Oh yes, of course. I hope you will join us one evening, Mr.—uh—Dorton. We will send a man to let you know the date."

Geoffrey had been dismissed. With a small sigh

of relief, he turned away only to find Miss Hartwell by his side.

"I will show Mr. Dorton the path back to Bradworth Hall," she said over her shoulder.

"Do not get any ideas, girl," her mother said, her eyes narrowed in warning.

Miss Hartwell rolled her eyes. "Honestly," she muttered and then made a show of taking Geoffrey's arm.

It was a short walk down the high street of Oakleigh to the point where the path to Bradworth entered a small wooded area. Miss Hartwell had dropped Geoffrey's arm as soon as they were out of sight of the vicarage and the two walked in silence for several minutes.

No sooner had they passed the last cottage on the dusty road, than a small pug scrambled over a hedgerow and threw itself at Miss Hartwell's knees, snuffling in transparent joy. The lady bent down and scooped up the dog, scratching it behind its quivering ears. "Georgie," she cooed at the wriggling beast. "What are you doing here?"

"Not yours, I take it." Geoffrey shook his head in disbelief.

"Well, no." Miss Hartwell placed a kiss between the pug's ears and set it back on the ground. "Go home," she said, giving it a pat on the rump.

"I assume its name is not Georgie, either." Geoffrey watched the squat figure disappear behind a hedge.

"Unlikely." Miss Hartwell shook her head. "He belongs to Miss Babson and I am quite sure she cannot remember his name. I know she cannot remember mine."

"I am certain I can find the path from here," Geoffrey said. "There is no need for you to go out of your way."

"No. It is no inconvenience and . . ." Miss Hartwell kicked a stone with her muddy half-boot and moved off down the street.

"And?" Geoffrey asked.

There followed another long silence, broken only by the rustling of the spring wind through the leaves, the occasional call of a thrush, and a sound that Geoffrey was sure was some dog preparing to accost them.

"Please forgive my mother," Miss Hartwell finally said. "She thinks I will make a cake of myself over every handsome man who comes my way."

"Handsome man?" Surprised, Geoffrey glanced quickly down at his companion.

"Oh!" Miss Hartwell's face flushed in a most attractive manner.

"Da—dash it," she said. "Oh well. Surely that is no surprise to you. You must have a mirror." She took a deep breath. "But the fact is that I do not make a cake of myself over men, handsome or otherwise."

"I take the hint."

Miss Hartwell stopped dead in the middle of the road and planted her hands on her hips. "Do not mistake me, Mr. Dorton. I no more believe you might make a cake of yourself over a short, plump spinster than I believe I would act in such a silly manner."

Geoffrey entered Bradworth Hall through the kitchen. Although Lord Marchbourn, his sister's husband, had insisted he stay at the Hall rather than the steward's cottage, Geoffrey did not want anyone near Oakleigh to know who he was. He was here to prove himself as a land manager and he could not do it if the inhabitants knew he was Geoffrey Dorrington, the Earl of Cheriton and heir to a dukedom.

Geoffrey's struggle to convince his politically powerful father that he was capable of more than lounging around London waiting to inherit was difficult enough without carrying the baggage of his inheritance into the effort with him. Anything he accomplished, he wanted to be because of his own abilities.

Lord Marchbourn, who had rescued him from a career of dissipation in London and set him on the road to estate management at his own estate in Somersetshire, had been only too happy to accept Geoffrey's offer to take full responsibility for Bradworth.

Sitting on a bench by the door to the kitchen garden, Geoffrey stripped off his jacket and tossed it out the door before tugging at his mud-caked boots. Lord, but he was a mess.

"Mr. Dorton, what happened to you?" Keys jingling at her waist, Mrs. Woodruff popped out of the pantry, dusting flour off her hands.

Geoffrey smiled at the woman who served as both cook and housekeeper for the under-inhabited hall. "I had a contretemps with a wolfhound. I'm afraid my jacket will need to be buried." He gestured in the direction of the open door.

Mrs. Woodruff leaned out the door, picked up the jacket, and immediately discarded it. "Ugh. Smells like you met the fish-eater."

"Ah, so you know Brummell." Geoffrey kicked off one boot and started on the other.

"Brummell, is it? Then I take it you've met our Miss Cassie as well."

"Yes. She rescued me from that oaf of a dog."

"The dog attacked you?" Mrs. Woodruff looked shocked.

"Not precisely. He tripped me, held me down, and

licked my face." Geoffrey grimaced and dragged his sleeve across his mouth at the memory.

"I am glad you've already met Miss Cassie. She's a plum. I'll just take these out back now, shall I?" Mrs. Woodruff picked up the boots and hurried out the door, leaving Geoffrey to consider how apt that description might be.

Chapter 2

Cassie took her time returning to the vicarage. She stopped to pick some primrose and campion that had blossomed in the hedgerows, holding the delicate buds to her face and inhaling the scent of spring. She chatted for a few moments with Miss Babson, who had come out of her cottage looking for her pug. Leaving her improvised posy with Miss Babson, she ambled the rest of the way home, not looking forward to her mother's inquisition about the new steward at Bradworth Hall.

The noise from the kitchen betokened an early supper and Cassie did not bother to see who was in there. She stuck her head into the library and found her father regarding his students with benign distress as they struggled through a translation of Homer. He looked up and winked at Cassie as she withdrew her head and started toward the stairs.

"Just where have you been, miss?" Mrs. Hartwell's voice rang out from the door to the small drawing room.

Cassie winced and turned toward her mother. "I have been talking with Miss Babson." This was no more than the truth although perhaps a little less.

Mrs. Hartwell sighed. "And playing with that

drooling dog of hers, I'll warrant. Come in here." She turned and walked back into the drawing room.

Cassie entered the snug little room and took her accustomed seat on the shabby settee in front of the west window. She fingered the worn damask cushion while she waited for her mother to take her own seat and pick up the needlework she had left beside her chair.

"So," said Mrs. Hartwell, jabbing her needle into the hapless linen she held in her hand. "Tell me about the steward."

"I cannot tell you very much, Mama. I met him crossing a field when I had to rescue him from Br— from Mr. Jenkins's wolfhound. It only seemed polite to introduce myself. What is it you wished to know?"

"I wish to know how long you spent with this young man today. Here." She leaned forward and handed her work basket to Cassie. "Make yourself useful."

Cassie extracted a stocking and a needle. She took her time threading the needle before answering her mother. "I pulled the dog off Mr. Dorton. We introduced ourselves and then he, very courteously, asked to accompany me so he could meet Papa. I have told you this, Mama."

"He is very handsome," Mrs. Hartwell said with exaggerated nonchalance.

"Yes, I suppose he is." Cassie bent over her work, knowing what was coming next.

"I expect more for you than a handsome face."

"Yes, Mama." Cassie squinted at the stocking in her hand and bit her lip to keep from saying more. She had heard this litany repeatedly since she came of age. Now, at twenty-seven and firmly on the shelf, she could not imagine why her mother persisted in thinking she would make a brilliant match or, indeed, any match at all. But her mother had planned the perfect match for each of her seven daughters as they came of age.

Although all of Cassie's older sisters had married, none had married the wealthy peer that Mrs. Hartwell envisioned for each of them. Cassie alone remained in the house, happy to take over her mother's housekeeping responsibilities, to care for her parents and her father's boarders, happy to spend the sunny afternoons tramping the fields on visits to her father's parishioners.

None of this deterred Mrs. Hartwell's scheming, and the news that Lord Marchbourn would not move into Bradworth Hall must have come as a severe blow.

"He is very handsome."

Cassie recognized her mother's neutral tone. She was determined to carry her point, and Cassie knew she must allow her to proceed if she was going to hear the end of it. "Yes, Mama. So you said."

"I thought you had noticed." Mrs. Hartwell set aside her sewing, focusing her attention on Cassie.

"Of course I noticed. Who would not?" Although Cassie would not admit it to her mother, when Mr. Dorton had finally been relieved of Brummell's importuning and clambered to his feet, her first glimpse of tanned face and sparkling blue eyes had quite taken her breath away.

"Do not get any ideas about him. He may be handsome, but he has nothing else to recommend him." Mrs. Hartwell glared at her youngest daughter.

Cassie sighed. She had lost count of the number of times she had had this particular conversation with her mother, although she imagined she could tot them up by counting the unmarried young men who had entered the county since she turned twenty.

Every time an unmarried man appeared, her mother warned her that they had no future and that Cassie had something better in store for her.

Cassie well knew what was in store for her: the life of a spinster, caring for her aging parents, probably followed by the life of a dependent sister, caring for nieces and nephews. But it had not been a hardship to follow her mother's advice. None of the young men appealed to her in the slightest.

"I would not upset yourself about Mr. Dorton, Mama. As you say, he is too handsome to be interested in someone like me. And, if I am not mistaken, too young. There must be at least a dozen young ladies in Oakleigh who will be in alt to meet the new steward."

"Do not underestimate yourself, girl."

Cassie dropped her head, examining the lumpy darn in the stocking she held. She knew she had gone one step too far and had triggered another familiar diatribe.

"You are very attractive, if a trifle short. And do not forget who your great-uncle is. A young man would do well to form an alliance with our family." Mrs. Hartwell fetched out her pincushion and stabbed her needle into it.

"Yes, Mama." Mrs. Hartwell never failed to bring up her uncle, the third Viscount Ripponden, during matrimonial discussions. Cassie had never laid eyes on the reclusive peer who spent all his time on his Yorkshire estate. Nor, to her knowledge, had anyone in her household ever corresponded with the gentleman. But her mother's consequence depended upon the connection, and she brought it up every time one of her daughters was of an age to marry. Now, with all her sisters married, Cassie was the repository of all her mother's pretensions.

* * *

"Cassie! Are you still upstairs?" Mrs. Hartwell's voice rang through the vicarage, and Cassie, indeed upstairs, was grateful that she had already risen and dressed. She put down the book she had been reading, rose from her window seat, and, puffing out a sigh of resignation, descended to the ground floor. Her mother sounded impatient, and her temper would not improve if Cassie dawdled.

Cassie came to a halt in the doorway to the front room. Sir Edmund Gilbert lounged on Mrs. Hartwell's best chair, a cup in one hand and buttered toast in the other. Sir Edmund was the second largest landowner in the area and the magistrate for this part of the county. And Cassie feared that, despite his advanced age, her mother might be envisioning him as a potential husband for her.

Stifling yet another sigh, Cassie squared her shoulders and joined her mother and her guest where they sat by the new windows overlooking the high street. "Sir Edmund." She dropped a perfunctory curtsey. "Mama."

"Sit and take tea with us, my dear." Mrs. Hartwell smiled happily up at Cassie. "Is it not delightful to see Sir Edmund so early in the day?"

Cassie gritted her teeth and forced a smile. "Indeed," she said, pouring herself a cup of tea from the pot in front of her mother and taking it to a straight-backed chair near the doorway. It would be more delightful to see the back of Sir Edmund.

The room was full west and the early spring sun had not yet crept in around the edges of the door to Mr. Hartwell's library. A thin, watery light filtered through the glass in back of Sir Edmund, highlighting his graying hair, heavily coated with pomade and, thank goodness, casting a shadow across his face. Cassie knew the gentleman well enough to be able to imagine his ruddy complexion and mud-colored eyes.

"Do you not wish to know why Sir Edmund is here, dearest?" Mrs. Hartwell gave her daughter a coaxing smile.

"Oh, of course," Cassie said, placing her cup on a side table and looking at Sir Edmund with feigned interest.

"A ball, my dear," the man said. "The very best kind of news for a young lady like yourself."

"A ball?" Cassie hesitated. She dearly loved to dance and there was little enough opportunity in Oakleigh, but she could not imagine that Sir Edmund would give a ball simply for the joy of pleasing his neighbors.

"May I ask the occasion?" Cassie retrieved her tea and reached for a piece of toast. Planting would begin soon and it seemed a peculiar time of year for a ball.

"Of course you may, my dear. Of course you may." Sir Edmund bared his yellowed teeth in an ingratiating smile. "My nephew's out from London. Sown his wild oats, y'know, and wants to learn his way around the place. Course you know he's the heir to Gilbert Grange." Sir Edmund's chest visibly expanded as he intoned the name of his estate.

Rodney Gilbert. He had spent several summers in Oakleigh when she was growing up. Cassie had no very fond memories of the boy, but merely nodded politely. "How nice for you, Sir Edmund."

"Is this not delightful news, Cassie?" Mrs. Hartwell interjected. "I remember how close you and young Master Rodney were as children."

Cassie searched her memory and could only remember how close she had come to punching young Master Rodney on the nose when they were children. He had been a dreadful little boy with a malicious streak that he bent upon anyone or anything that happened to be available.

"Hmm, yes, Mama. I remember Mr. Gilbert well."

"And now you must promise to lead the ball with him." Sir Edmund turned his earnest expression on Mrs. Hartwell. "She must promise."

"Of course she will," Mrs. Hartwell said, shooting Cassie a warning glance as her daughter opened her mouth to protest.

"Of course I will," Cassie echoed.

Cassie was on her knees in the herb garden, preparing the earth for new planting. It was her job and her pleasure to tend this part of the garden. She sat back on her heels and inhaled deeply. She loved the smell of the rich damp earth in the spring and the feel of the newly turned soil under her fingers.

She looked around with an air of satisfaction. Over the years, she had enlarged the plot to include not only the plants used in cooking and medicine, but those she loved simply for themselves. She gently touched a young orris shoot and, looking at the section she had added last year, chuckled. The plants in this area, chaste tree, meadow rue, and wild strawberry, were those medieval gardeners associated with love and marriage. For a moment, she wondered if it was strange to jest with plants.

Cassie's gaze remained riveted on the chaste tree, calling up the purple blossoms of last summer. Suddenly, the image of a golden head rose between her and the garden. Mr. Dorton, young, vital, and—yes—handsome.

Cassie shook her head. The new steward had no business in her daydreams. Her mother would be seriously displeased to find him there.

"Cassie!" As if conjured by her daughter, Mrs. Hartwell appeared at Cassie's side.

"What are you doing out here staring into the distance? What if Sir Edmund should see you sitting on the ground woolgathering? He would think you were addled."

"Did Sir Edmund not leave an hour ago?" Cassie gathered up her tools and stood before her mother, brushing off the skirt of her apron.

"Yes, he is gone, but he might have been here. And you know you must make a good impression on him." Mrs. Hartwell cast a critical eye over Cassie's gardening clothes. "You look like a servant."

"I look like I have been working in the garden, Mama. And I do not understand why you persist in thinking that Sir Edmund is an eligible *parti*. He must be nearly Papa's age."

Mrs. Hartwell widened her eyes in a look of pure exasperation. "Young and handsome will not put a roof over your head, my girl. Leastways the kind of roof you deserve to have. But I am no longer thinking of Sir Edmund."

Cassie brightened. "Thank you, Mama. It is good to hear that."

"No, no. I am now thinking of Mr. Rodney Gilbert. He is more nearly your age and will one day be a baronet and landowner."

"Not Rodney." Cassie set her jaw in a stubborn line and stared at her mother.

"What do you mean? You have not seen him since he was twelve." Mrs. Hartwell took Cassie by the shoulders and turned her around so that she could untie her apron.

"I mean," said Cassie over her shoulder, "that he was an odious boy at twelve and I am certain he is still odious."

"Nonsense. You have not seen him in fifteen years. He will be a fine gentleman." Her expression somber, Mrs. Hartwell turned her daughter back around to face her.

Keeping her hands on her daughter's shoulders, she looked intently into Cassie's eyes as if to impart the seriousness of her next statement. "This will be your last chance, Cassie. We could not give you a season, and if Lord Marchbourn does not mean to come to Bradworth Hall, your only opportunity to marry well will be Mr. Gilbert. Do not throw it away."

Cassie shrugged out of her apron and, leaving the garment hanging on her mother's hands, ran into the house.

Cassie tore by her father and his students and up the stairs. She flung open the door to her room and came to a dead stop. How foolish. She was not a young miss to have an attack of temper at something she did not wish to hear. She had meant to throw herself on her bed, but as she stood in the middle of her whitewashed floor and looked at the mended coverlet on her bed, she realized that her mother wanted her to be happy. And her mother believed that marriage to a comfortable fortune would give her that happiness. Perhaps she was right.

Chapter 3

It did not occur to Geoffrey that he had been thinking about Cassie Hartwell until he saw her again. But the moment she came into view, it was as if he had been waiting for her ever since he'd left her.

He was in Oakleigh trying to hire additional workers for the spring planting. As he was late to Devonshire, unemployed workers were thin on the ground. But he had happily found several younger sons at loose ends in the Blue Unicorn and was quite satisfied with his mission.

As Geoffrey stepped out of the tavern, he very nearly ran over Miss Hartwell, who had just stepped out of Clark's store with a string-tied parcel under her arm. Bringing himself up short, Geoffrey bowed.

"Miss Hartwell. How delightful to see you again." He looked down the street and then back into Miss Hartwell's laughing eyes.

"I see what you are doing, Mr. Dorton," she said, cocking her head at him. "You are looking for dogs, aren't you?"

Geoffrey grinned. "What use is there denying it? It was humiliating enough to be pinned by your friend Brummell in the middle of a field. I do not care to repeat the experience here in view of all of Oakleigh. May I take your parcel?"

"Oh." Miss Hartwell looked down at her package. "I thank you, but I am not going directly home. I have several more errands to accomplish."

"As I have accomplished mine, I am completely at your service." Geoffrey removed the package from Miss Hartwell's hands and tucked it under his arm.

"Shall we?" Geoffrey offered Miss Hartwell his other arm.

Cassie Hartwell looked delightfully flustered, but, after a slight hesitation, slipped her hand into the crook of Geoffrey's arm.

"I warn you, sir," she said, smiling merrily, "I dawdle in the shops."

"Do you indeed, Miss Hartwell? I look forward to the experience." Just having the lady on his arm made Geoffrey feel like smiling. Even as he walked down Oakleigh High Street with Cassie Hartwell on his arm, Geoffrey knew that he should run for home. There was no future in keeping company with a vicar's daughter. He was only likely to raise expectations that would come to naught.

Rather than run, however, Geoffrey put his qualms aside and followed Cassie into Mr. Tibbet's shop. The draper's establishment was small but well stocked with many different fabrics. A far cry, Geoffrey thought, from the fashionable shops on Regent Street where the linen draper would no more stock woolens than the milliner would carry boots.

Mr. Tibbet looked up as the bell over his door rang. "Miss Cassie." The wrinkled face broke into a wide smile. "What brings you here today?"

"I have a commission from my mother." Miss Hartwell dropped Geoffrey's arm and moved toward the counter.

"Have you brought us a beau?" Mr. Tibbet asked, nodding at Geoffrey, who was shifting uncomfortably by the door.

"Oh my." Miss Hartwell blushed, her hand flying to her cheek. "Oh, your pardon. Mr. Tibbet, this is Mr. Dorton, the new steward at Bradworth."

"Oh, aye, Miss Cassie. I know who he is. My question was not that." The shopkeeper winked at Geoffrey.

"Now, stop that. Mr. Dorton is assuredly not my beau. He was kind enough to escort me on my errands, and I will not have you plaguing the poor man. We do not want him to regret his gallantry, do we?" Miss Hartwell shook her head in mock exasperation and began examining the bolts of fabric that lined the shop.

Geoffrey crossed the room and leaned against the counter, watching his companion compare material that all looked exactly the same to him. He admired the play of sunlight on her lightly tanned skin as she held a length of muslin up to the window. She was so different from the pale beauties of his acquaintance in London. Most of them would be appalled to display any indication that they had been out in the sun. It seemed to Geoffrey that they were entirely mistaken. The sun had given Cassie Hartwell a glow that no amount of paint could emulate.

"She's a prime 'un, our Miss Cassie," Mr. Tibbet said softly.

Geoffrey, pulled from reverie, glanced at the man on the other side of the counter.

"Look at her." The shopkeeper shot Geoffrey an assessing glance and then lifted his chin toward the window. "More to her than just that pretty face. Thrifty, she is, and resourceful. There would be no waste in any home she ran. Make some man a fine wife."

Geoffrey watched Miss Hartwell run her hand over the fabric, hoping she was far enough from the counter to miss Mr. Tibbet's pointed remarks.

The shopkeeper drew a deep breath, but before he could continue, Geoffrey nodded politely and moved away from the counter, joining Miss Hartwell in her perusal of the wares.

"I told you I dawdled." She smiled up at him as she replaced the bolt of fabric she had been examining. "You must not feel you have to remain with me. I do this all the time without an escort.

"I will take two yards of this, Mr. Tibbet." She patted the fabric on the table and then turned back to Geoffrey. "My mother is very particular and I dare not go home with shoddy goods."

Geoffrey nodded, suddenly aware that he might have put himself into a difficult situation, unsure what to say. Was every merchant they visited going to attempt to make a match between Miss Hartwell and the new steward? Did Miss Hartwell think of him as a possible suitor?

Seeing no way to renege on his offer of escort, Geoffrey gravely accompanied Miss Hartwell back to the street.

"Is there some problem, Mr. Dorton?" Geoffrey and his companion had stopped before the Blue Unicorn while she consulted her list. Folding the paper, she turned her clear green eyes on Geoffrey.

He cleared his throat, searching for a graceful exit from his impulsive offer.

"Miss Hartwell, Mr. Dorton." The booming voice of Sir Edmund Gilbert interrupted Geoffrey's proposed flight.

"Sir Edmund." Geoffrey and his companion

spoke in unison, executing the proper acknowl-
edgments as they did so.

Sir Edmund drew forward the young man who ac-
companied him. "Rodney, allow me to present Mr.
Dorton to you. He is the new steward at Bradworth.
And I'm sure you remember Cassie—Miss Hartwell.
Mr. Dorton, m'nephew, Mr. Rodney Gilbert."

Mr. Rodney Gilbert ignored Geoffrey. He bowed
to Miss Hartwell, his gaze flowing familiarly over
her person. Geoffrey took an instant dislike to him.

"Miss Hartwell." The man's voice was as oily as
his appearance. "How delightful that we meet
again. Perhaps you will join us in our little jaunt
through Oakleigh."

Miss Hartwell shot a quick glance at Geoffrey,
who immediately comprehended the problem.

"Miss Hartwell has honored me with her company this afternoon," he said, wincing inwardly at
what this little speech might convey to both Sir Edmund and Miss Hartwell.

"Hmmm." Mr. Gilbert looked at Geoffrey for the
first time. "If that is Miss Hartwell's desire, my uncle
and I will continue our tour on our own. But I will
be in the neighborhood for some time. Gilbert
Grange will be mine one day, you know, and I intend to reacquaint myself with the environs. I trust
Miss Hartwell will find some time for me in her
busy schedule."

As Geoffrey waited for the beaming Sir Edmund
and his encroaching nephew to move away, his
companion moved a little closer to him and took
his arm.

"Thank you," she whispered, once the Gilberts had
entered the inn. "I never could abide that man."

"You know Mr. Gilbert, then?" Geoffrey turned

his head to watch the men until they entered the Blue Unicorn.

"Knew him as a boy, rather. He was dreadful then and I cannot but think that age has not improved him." Miss Hartwell glanced back over her shoulder as if to ascertain that the gentlemen were not following them.

"But I do thank you. I think you were about to take your leave when Sir Edmund appeared."

Geoffrey was startled. Was he so transparent?

"I assure you, Miss Hartwell . . . I had no . . . I mean . . ."

"Never mind." The young lady had obviously decided to take pity on him. "I appreciate your kindness and assure you that you will not be made to pay for it."

Later, sitting behind the steward's desk at Bradworth, Geoffrey found himself unable to concentrate on the ledger in front of him. Cassie Hartwell's words of assurance rang through his mind and he wondered once again if he had, indeed, escaped an inappropriate attraction.

Geoffrey watched the sun set outside the small office. The room was bare except for the desk, a few chairs, and the shelves holding ledgers, agricultural journals, and a few books. It had been a warm day and no fire was lit. An evening chill began to pervade the room.

Geoffrey stood and pulled on his jacket, smiling as he recalled the morning's shopping expedition. The face of every merchant in Oakleigh had lit when Miss Hartwell entered their shops. And it was obviously not because of her extravagant custom. Indeed, Cassie Hartwell was a careful and frugal

shopper, and if she dawdled, it was in the service of
making the best bargain she could. With each carefully considered purchase Geoffrey was made more
aware of the gulf between Miss Hartwell's world
and the one he inhabited.

Except for this moment, he reminded himself,
sitting back down at the desk and pulling the
leather-bound volume toward him. Right now he
was the steward of the Bradworth estate and, as far
as the inhabitants of Oakleigh were concerned, important only as he represented his master, Lord
Marchbourn.

Cassie Hartwell might very well consider Mr. Geoffrey Dorton, land steward, suitable as a potential husband. And that way lay disaster, for a vicar's daughter
would never be a suitable wife for the future Duke of
Passmore. Although he had enjoyed her company
today, Geoffrey knew that he had better be circumspect about any attentions he paid Miss Hartwell.

And leave her to the attentions of Mr. Rodney
Gilbert? Geoffrey felt the back of his neck prickle
as he recalled the appraising look Mr. Gilbert had
given Miss Hartwell. As if he were contemplating
the pleasures of that lush little body. The thought
did not sit well. Geoffrey tried to convince himself
that whatever took place between Miss Cassie
Hartwell and Mr. Rodney Gilbert was none of his affair, but he could not seem to overcome his distaste
for the idea.

The sun was close to the horizon and the room too
dark to focus on the neat columns of figures Geoffrey had been recording. He gave up for the night
and, retrieving the pile of correspondence on the
corner of the desk, left the block of estate offices and
crossed the back garden toward the house.

Geoffrey stopped in the middle of the garden

and sat heavily on the rim of the stone fountain. He absently picked at the dried lichen encrusting the edge and thought that he ought to reestablish the water source before Julian visited his new holding.

Julian, Lord Marchbourn, would probably not choose to come to Devonshire until the planting at Marchbourn was safely completed. Then he and his wife, Sarah, Geoffrey's sister, would likely arrive to see what his cousin had left him.

Geoffrey was grateful for the opportunity to prove himself as an estate manager out from under the careful supervision of his brother-in-law. And he was grateful for the opportunity to prove himself capable of anything away from the ever-critical eye of his father, the Duke of Passmore.

Geoffrey had a momentary vision of presenting the vicar's daughter to his father. The duke had only recently recovered from Sarah's marriage to a farmer baron. A country-bred daughter with no aristocratic blood would give him an apoplexy regardless of how genteel the lady. Much as he longed to prove himself apart from his father, Geoffrey did not wish to drive the duke to his grave.

Chapter 4

Cassie squinted at her reflection. If she narrowed her eyes to just a slit, she looked quite pretty. The pale blue silk gown was a year out of date, but still lovely. The newer fashion for a slightly dropped waist suited Cassie's short, rounded body. The raised lines of two years ago had made her look as if she were all bosom. The waistline and the blessed lack of ruffles were much more flattering.

She was grateful that her mother paid attention to current fashion. Although Mrs. Hartwell was a careful manager of her husband's income, she had always taken care to present her daughters in the best possible light. But even a marriage-minded mama could not afford a new gown every year, particularly when the opportunities to wear it were so thin.

Cassie lifted her hands to her hair. Too curly to be fashioned into anything presentable when it was long, short it formed a sort of permanent nimbus around her head, which she considered the lesser of two evils.

Cassie pulled on her gloves and joined her mother in the front entry.

"You look well tonight, Cassie." Mrs. Hartwell signaled for her daughter to turn. "Yes. Although current fashions will never look as well on you as they do on Eleanor, you will do quite nicely."

Cassie rolled her eyes. Nothing looked as well on her as it did on her sister Eleanor. She did not mention that the dress was not quite current. If it gave her mother comfort to think so, she was happy to oblige.

"Thank you, Mama." She dropped a curtsey whose irony she was certain was lost on her mother.

"Is Papa escorting us?" Cassie looked around the hallway, but saw no sign of her father.

Mrs. Hartwell sighed. "Naturally not. Your father has an important tome to look into tonight. It will not wait."

Cassie smiled. "No, it never will, will it?"

"Sir Edmund is sending his coach around for us. Is that not kind?" Mrs. Hartwell peered out the window. "It should be here any moment."

"Yes, remarkably civil." Cassie pulled at her gloves, trying to allay the idea of being beholden in any way to Sir Edmund and his nephew.

Mrs. Hartwell reached out to fluff her daughter's right sleeve and, while she was there, adjust the bodice of her gown a shade higher. She stood back to survey her work and then plucked at one of the shiny brown curls falling against Cassie's forehead.

"Mind your tongue tonight, miss. You are entirely too acute." Mrs. Hartwell examined her daughter for a second time. "Mr. Gilbert is likely the last chance you will have to marry well."

"I do not like Mr. Gilbert." Cassie lifted her chin.

"You do not know Mr. Gilbert," her mother said.

"I know him well enough to know I do not wish to marry him."

"Hmmph!" Mrs. Hartwell returned her gaze to

the window. "Too acute," she muttered, "too opinionated, too long on the shelf. What am I to do with you?"

Cassie toed the worn rug in front of the door, trying to suppress a spurt of rebelliousness. "You might let me make my own decisions."

"Oh, indeed." Mrs. Hartwell spun around to face her daughter, hands on her hips. "And if I did, what would happen? You would end your days a spinster dependent on your sisters' husbands." She narrowed her eyes at Cassie. "Or are you thinking of the handsome new steward?"

"I am thinking I am old enough to make up my own mind," Cassie answered promptly. But she flushed as she said it, wondering if perhaps she did have Mr. Dorton in the back of her mind.

"You will do as I . . ."

Mrs. Hartwell broke off as the Gilbert carriage pulled up in front of the vicarage. Cassie gave a silent prayer of thanks and held the door for her mother.

Gilbert Grange had no ballroom, but Sir Edmund had improvised by clearing his large drawing room of furniture and throwing open the French windows to the back terrace where lanterns hung among the trees and arbors. It was possible to dance from the drawing room onto the terrace if one was careful not to trip on the sills.

When Cassie and her mother entered, dancing had not yet begun and the assembled group milled about the drawing room, greeting each other and eyeing the open windows with some concern.

"Mrs. Hartwell, Miss Hartwell. How delightful to see you here." Sir Edmund hurried through the crowd and bowed to the ladies. "I trust your journey was pleasant," he added, looking pleased with himself.

"Indeed, Sir Edmund. We thank you for your kindness in sending your carriage."

"Not at all. Not at all. Must have Miss Cassie here to open the ball. Now where is that boy?" Sir Edmund looked around the room.

"Looking for me, Uncle?" Rodney Gilbert appeared at Sir Edmund's elbow. "Ah, Miss Hartwell." He bowed. "How charming to meet you again. And can this lovely young woman be your mother?"

Cassie watched her mother beam at this blatant Spanish coin and groaned to herself. The evening was not beginning well at all.

"Well, well, now that you're here, m'dear, we can begin the festivities."

Cassie cast a quick glance around the room and then down at last year's gown. She shrugged. This was the depths of Devonshire, not a London ballroom. How bad could it be?

She looked back into the room, assuring herself that these were all people she had known from childhood. Then a figure stepped through the windows from the terrace and her heart stopped.

Of course Mr. Dorton would be here. He was new, but he was now part of the neighborhood, and Sir Edmund seemed to have invited everyone with the least toehold in gentility. Now that she considered it, Cassie realized that she had known all along he would be here and that was probably why she had fussed so about her gown.

Was there any reason, however, for him to be so impossibly handsome? He was not the most fashionably dressed gentleman in the room. She supposed that would be Rodney Gilbert in his high collar points and flamboyant waistcoat. But he was the handsomest. He wore trousers as most young men did these days. They, like his jacket, were a brilliant black, contrasting with the sparkling white of his linen and the soft cream of his waistcoat. Suddenly she felt hopelessly dowdy.

While Cassie stood, rooted to the floor, Sir Edmund signaled the three musicians in the far corner. As they began tuning their instruments, he took Cassie's hand and gave it to his nephew. "Call the dance, my dear."

Cassie flushed a deep scarlet as she recalled where she was and what she was expected to do. "Call the dance?" she asked faintly.

Her mother, standing close behind her, gave her a covert poke in the ribs.

"Yes, of course," Cassie said with an unnaturally bright smile. "Let us have the Country Bumpkin."

"Cassie!" Her mother's voice hissed in her ear.

"The Country Bumpkin, Mama. It seems most appropriate."

Sir Edmund walked off to give instructions to his small orchestra, and Cassie allowed Mr. Gilbert to take her hand and lead her to the head of the set that was forming. From the corner of her eye, she saw Geoffrey Dorton leading Alice Morton to the bottom of the line.

"Is something amiss?" Although they were in place at the head of the dance, Rodney Gilbert had not yet released Cassie's hand. The pressure on her fingers recalled her attention to her own partner.

Cassie shook her head. "No, nothing, Mr. Gilbert. I am simply unused to being singled out for such an honor."

"Ah." Mr. Gilbert's self-satisfied smile widened. "Perhaps you would like to become accustomed to it."

"No. No indeed. I do not believe I should like that at all." The musicians struck up the tune, and Cassie turned to the second gentleman to begin the dance.

As Cassie progressed down the dance, the moment inevitably arrived when she found her gloved hand enclosed by Geoffrey Dorton's larger one. As he turned her toward the next figure, she smiled up at him. He returned her regard with a solemn nod and released her to the next gentleman. Cassie finished the dance and the one that followed, puzzled by Mr. Dorton's curt acknowledgment.

Once the set was over, Cassie's distraction was such that she was surprised to find herself at the French windows. The cool evening air wafted across her cheeks, and she suddenly realized that Mr. Gilbert was escorting her onto the terrace.

She removed her hand from Mr. Gilbert's arm and stepped back. "I must find my mother," Cassie said, looking back into the room. "Has she gone into the garden?"

"I have no idea." The gentleman looked unconcerned about the location of Mrs. Hartwell. "Shall we go out and look for her?" He set Cassie's hand back on his arm and stepped over the threshold.

"Are you seeking your mother, Miss Hartwell?" The deep voice of Geoffrey Dorton sounded from somewhere over Cassie's left shoulder. She turned, disconcerted at the way her heart tripped upon hearing it.

"Yes, Mr. Dorton. Have you seen her?" Cassie's voice sounded unnaturally breathless in her own ears.

"I have," Geoffrey said, then nodded at Cassie's escort. "Mr. Gilbert."

"Dorton." Rodney Gilbert gave a single nod.

"We have no need of your assistance," he said. "I am perfectly capable of returning Miss Hartwell to her mother."

"Indeed?" Geoffrey raised an eyebrow. "Then perhaps you should be leading her toward the chaperones rather than outdoors."

"Mind your own business, Dorton." Gilbert reached for Cassie's hand, but she had already placed it on Geoffrey Dorton's arm.

"I would be grateful if you will take me there, Mr. Dorton." Cassie took only a moment to thank Rodney Gilbert for the dance before turning her back on him and allowing Geoffrey to lead her across the floor.

Lines were forming for another set and Cassie wondered if Mr. Dorton would ask her to dance. She looked at the dancers and then quickly up at her escort. But he seemed determined to avoid the dance and steered Cassie toward the perimeter, his eyes straight ahead and his expression grim.

So, they would not be dancing. Cassie tried to smother her disappointment. Granted, she was a vicar's daughter in last year's dress. But it seemed unreasonable for a land steward to act as though he was above her touch, regardless of how handsome and well dressed he was.

Cassie softly fingered the sleeve beneath her hand. Not only was the jacket cut as though it was made for the man, the fabric was of a quality rarely seen in the environs of Oakleigh. Lord Marchbourn must be a generous employer.

"Mr. Dorton, I . . ." Cassie glanced up at her escort's face and her thoughts fled. His handsome face was locked in a mask of stern concentration. If Cassie had not seen him laugh, she would have said that this was the face of a man who did not know how.

"Miss Hartwell?" Mr. Dorton slowed and looked down at Cassie. "Is there something you wish to say?"

They were approaching the chaperones. "I . . . I thank you for the escort." Cassie felt flustered and wondered what she had been going to say.

"I am happy to be of service." Mr. Dorton bowed to Mrs. Hartwell and to Cassie and removed to another corner of the room.

"Where is Mr. Gilbert?" Mrs. Hartwell did not look pleased.

"I believe he is over there." Cassie gestured toward the center of the room where several couples were essaying a sprightly reel.

Mrs. Hartwell narrowed her eyes. "What were you doing with the steward when you should have returned to me with your partner?"

"I was doing just that—returning to you," Cassie said. "Mr. Gilbert was determined that we should look for you in the garden. Mr. Dorton forestalled him and brought me here."

"Hmmph." Mrs. Hartwell slanted another narrow-eyed glance at her daughter. "Do not slight a baronet's heir for a handsome face, my girl. Your future may depend upon it."

Cassie took the seat beside her mother without answering. She looked across the room at Mr. Dorton, who had engaged another young lady and was taking his place in a set.

As Cassie sat running her hand over the ribbon trimming the skirt of her gown, she finally admitted to herself that she had come to Gilbert Grange hoping to dance with Geoffrey Dorton. She had enjoyed his company each time they met and thought that he enjoyed hers.

The dance was apparently not to be. Cassie fought down an unreasonable agitation. Geoffrey

Dorton was nothing to her but a recent acquaintance. How dare he be so friendly on the high street of Oakleigh and snub her in the squire's drawing room? Why did he bother to rescue her from Rodney Gilbert's misdirection if he was going to ignore her otherwise?

Cassie sat through to the end of the set and then could not sit still any longer. Her state demanded movement. "I am going to fetch a cool drink, Mama. Shall I bring you one?"

"You should not be going for refreshments." Mrs. Hartwell looked disapproving.

"If I do not, we are likely to expire from thirst," Cassie said. "I do not see anyone else offering to do so."

"Bring me ratafia, then, and do not dawdle." Mrs. Hartwell pulled out her fan and sat back in her chair.

The route to the refreshments table took Cassie by the open French windows. The fragrant breeze of a cool spring evening wafted through the door, carrying the green scent of a Devonshire spring and the perfume of early-blooming flowers. The full moon reflected in the small pool at the far end of the garden and the dim terrace seemed a welcome respite from the heat of the drawing room and the warmth of her anger. Looking quickly around to see if anyone was watching, Cassie slipped out the door.

And straight into the hard, superfine-clad chest of Geoffrey Dorton.

"Oof."

Cassie tottered back and Mr. Dorton's hands closed on her shoulders, steadying her.

"Miss Hartwell," Mr. Dorton said, his tone threaded with irony.

"Oh!" Cassie could feel herself blush right up to the roots of her hair. "Oh, forgive me. I did not . . ."

"You did not follow me out here?" Geoffrey asked.

"No!" Cassie, placed her palms against his chest and pushed. "How dare you imply . . ."

Mr. Dorton's hands tightened on her arms and Cassie gave up the idea of freeing herself until he was done taunting her. "How dare you? I came out here for a breath of air."

"Hmmm." Cassie heard the doubt in that one syllable.

"If you find my company distasteful, Mr. Dorton, you need only tell me so and I will be happy to avoid you at all costs."

Hoping that no more need be said, Cassie tried to pull out of Geoffrey Dorton's grasp.

"No." The word seemed wrenched from him in a harsh expiration. His grip tightened and the next thing Cassie knew she was flush against that broad chest and Mr. Dorton's lips were on hers.

The kiss was hard and fast. Cassie barely had time to feel the warm strength of his mouth and imbibe the smoky flavor of his skin before it was over. As quickly as it had begun, the kiss was over and Geoffrey Dorton was striding across the garden toward the back gate. As quickly as it had begun, Cassie's anger was gone, replaced entirely by longing and confusion.

Chapter 5

"Damn, damn, damn." Geoffrey had removed his gloves and was beating them against his thigh as he strode across the field separating Gilbert Grange from Bradworth. He had left everything else at the Grange: his cloak, his hat, his horse.

He swore again. This time imagining the scene tomorrow when he must return to retrieve his belongings.

"Damn!" A rabbit, flushed by his tramping, skittered through the damp grass and across his path. Geoffrey looked down at his feet. He was ruining a good pair of shoes as well.

What had possessed him to kiss Cassie Hartwell? Geoffrey shook his head and continued striding through the field. The soft mist of late evening created a corona around the full moon and dropped a fine veil over the landscape, almost obscuring the trees at the edge of the open land. But there was light enough for Geoffrey to make his way over the uncertain terrain, and he was grateful for it.

He had contemplated not attending the ball, but a good land steward must be on excellent terms with the neighboring landowners. He had determined, however, that he would pay less attention to

Miss Hartwell. This would be the place to put paid
to any notion that the steward was courting the
vicar's daughter. Anyone who might have seen
them together in Oakleigh would now see that he
did not single her out for his particular attentions.

It had seemed such a good idea until the moment she smiled up at him during the first set. Even
now, Geoffrey's heart turned over at the memory of
that warm smile. But he had held to his plan even
when he had rescued her from an unsought stroll
in the garden and returned her to her mother. He
knew she wanted to dance with him, and Lord, how
he longed to offer. But a small hurt now, he told
himself, would save them both a more serious
wound later.

And what was the result? He had gone outside because it had become difficult to see Cassie Hartwell
and not ask her to dance. When she ran into him—
and he had to admit that it had been an accident—
he accused her of following him, kissed her, and
ran away.

"Damn!"

Geoffrey was almost on Bradworth land when his
nostrils were assailed by the distinct odor of fish.

"Oh no." He did not even have to look. The smell
and the accompanying sound of large paws gallop-
ing through the field were enough.

"Brummell." Geoffrey hoped his voice sounded
both friendly and commanding, and apparently, it
did. The huge wolfhound slowed his pace and
padded up to Geoffrey, nudging his hand with a
cold, fishy nose.

Geoffrey patted the rough head, thinking that
this was, at least, better than being licked. The dog
snuffled his hand and fell into step beside Geoffrey

as he continued toward the hedgerow separating Gilbert's land from Bradworth's.

Despite the smell, Geoffrey began to enjoy having a companion on his flight from the ball. Brummell seemed content to trot along at Geoffrey's side, ranging out occasionally to sniff at something invisible to Geoffrey, but obviously of interest to the dog. Perhaps fish were lurking in the undergrowth.

Returning from a foray, Brummell gave a small leap. Geoffrey flinched, but the dog simply grinned at him and took up his former position. Geoffrey closed his eyes for a second, remembering his first meeting with the shaggy beast and, he need hardly remind himself, his first meeting with Cassie Hartwell.

The heavy dew mantling the untended field had soaked through Geoffrey's dancing shoes and fine stockings. He would have to send to London for another pair of shoes or give up dancing. At the moment, the latter seemed like the better idea. He should have stayed away from the ball. He should have danced with all the local ladies, including Cassie Hartwell, and he should have taken himself off to the card room to woo the local landowners as any good steward would.

He definitely should not have kissed Cassie Hartwell in a darkened corner of the terrace and taken off like a frightened schoolboy. He had no idea how he would ever face the lady again and fervently hoped that no one else had seen them. "Damn!"

Brummell stopped snuffling the ground to give Geoffrey an interrogatory glance.

"I wasn't talking to you," Geoffrey told him before recalling that the dog wouldn't understand.

Brummell seemed indifferent to whether or not the exclamation was addressed to him and took the opportunity to sidle closer to Geoffrey and shove his nose into Geoffrey's palm again.

"You don't care." Geoffrey stopped a moment to stroke the smelly muzzle under his hand. "All you care about is fish and affection. And if I weren't here to give you one or the other, you would just find someone else."

Brummell woofed happily, apparently in complete agreement with Geoffrey's observation.

"Hmmm." Geoffrey resumed his pace, his thoughts circling around what he had just said to the dog. Perhaps that was just the way to avoid further complications. It looked as though the squire's nephew was bent on courting Miss Hartwell. If Geoffrey just stayed out of the way for a while, surely Mr. Rodney Gilbert would win the day.

As Geoffrey climbed the stile between Sir Edmund's land and the Bradford estate, the image of Cassie Hartwell being urged onto the terrace by the oily Rodney Gilbert flashed through his mind. He stopped with one foot on the step and shuddered. She hadn't liked it, and neither had Geoffrey. Surely, Cassie Hartwell would rebuff any attentions from that quarter. Nevertheless, Geoffrey's blood boiled at the very thought of Rodney Gilbert laying a finger on her.

Cassie lingered on the terrace, her fingers pressed against her lips and her heart thumping erratically. The figure of Geoffrey Dorton had long since disappeared into the darkness at the edge of Sir Edmund's back garden, but her eyes remained fixed to the point where the black-clad figure had finally merged with night. She could barely breathe. What had happened?

"Miss Cassie?" Sir Edmund stepped through the door and peered around the terrace.

"Here, sir." Cassie could hear the little squeak in her own voice and blushed into the shadows. She hesitated a moment before stepping forward.

"There you are, my dear. Your mama is looking for you. And so, might I add, is a certain young man." Sir Edmund winked and held out his arm. Cassie was compelled to let him lead her back into the drawing room.

"Where have you been?" Mrs. Hartwell pulled Cassie down into the chair next to hers and retained her grip on Cassie's arm.

"On the terrace. I needed some air. It is perishing hot in here."

"Alone?" Mrs. Hartwell's grasp tightened until Cassie winced and pried her mother's fingers loose.

"Alone," she said, trying very hard to keep her tone neutral and her color normal. She was not certain she had been successful at either.

"Where is Mr. Dorton?" Mrs. Hartwell peered around the room. Cassie knew what her mother suspected and hoped that she didn't know he had been on the terrace.

"I really couldn't say, Mama. Did you wish me to watch him?"

"Don't be pert, young lady. I don't see him in the room and I don't trust him. He is too handsome by half and no doubt expects every young lady in the neighborhood to be at his beck and call."

Cassie shrugged.

"I expect," her mother continued, "that you will not be so foolish. It can only lead to heartache."

Mrs. Hartwell released Cassie's arm, apparently satisfied that she had made her point. Cassie nodded and edged back in her chair.

Heartache. In that Mama was probably right. An infatuation with Geoffrey Dorton would likely lead to nothing but heartache. No doubt, someone with his beauty would eventually go to London and find a beautiful wife with an equally beautiful dowry. Anything that happened between them while he was here would be in the nature of a diversion. And Cassie had no intention of being anyone's diversion.

And yet . . . Her heart had not yet resumed its normal rhythm and her lips still felt the imprint of Geoffrey's sudden kiss. What had he meant by it? What was she to think? Cassie shook her head, trying to clear away any thought of that confusing encounter on the terrace.

"Are you engaged for the waltz?" Rodney Gilbert appeared before Cassie, bowing low and looking as though he expected she had saved it for him.

Cassie drew a sudden breath, preparing to tell him she would not dance again tonight, when her mother spoke up. "She has been hoping you would ask, Mr. Gilbert."

Cassie muffled a squeak before nodding at the man before her and rising to dance. As she accompanied Rodney Gilbert to the floor, she threw a speaking look over her shoulder, promising her mother retribution for the latest of her surreptitious pokes in the ribs. She wouldn't be surprised if she was black and blue as the result of her mother's matchmaking.

Cassie was surprised to find the waltz not as repellant as she had anticipated. Although she would have preferred not to have been touched at all by Rodney Gilbert, he did hold her at a respectable distance and managed not to breathe directly in her face. Small mercies, but mercies nonetheless.

She could not, however, help but compare the

dance with what it might have been had Geoffrey
Dorton been her partner. The weave of Mr. Gilbert's jacket felt uneven to fingers that had recently
touched the finer fabric of Mr. Dorton's sleeve. The
starched shirt points seemed dingier than Mr. Dorton's less imposing collar. The red and gold waistcoat screamed at eyes that would rather have rested
on a delicate cream.

But, most of all, Cassie longed for the hand at her
waist to be someone else's, longed for her hand to
rest on a stronger, broader shoulder, longed to look
into eyes that were blue as the Devonshire sky and
that smiled at her even when Mr. Dorton was somber.

"Excellent. I shall call for you in the afternoon."

Oh Lord. She had been daydreaming and entirely missed what Mr. Gilbert had said. Had she just
agreed to go somewhere with Rodney Gilbert?

"Er . . . what time will that be?" Cassie desperately
hoped for a clue to the plan.

"About one o'clock, I should think. The dogs will
have had their run by then and be more biddable."

Dogs. She had agreed to see Mr. Gilbert's dogs.
Well, that would not be so bad. Perhaps she was
wrong about Mr. Gilbert as well. A man who liked
dogs must have some good qualities. And anything was preferable to mooning over a chance
kiss in the dark.

"One o'clock will be fine."

Chapter 6

The Bradworth fields needed attention. The old man had been too sick to attend to them for the past two years and his steward had obviously been negligent. Like most of the countryside, the fields had been enclosed, but the tenants had been shamefully neglected in the process. There was no excuse for that. It was his job to rectify all of it.

His job. Geoffrey drew his horse to a stop at the top of a rise overlooking the Bradworth estate. He smiled as his eyes swept over the green pastures, the newly dug ditches, and the baby hedgerows. He had not been raised to have a job. He had been raised to follow his father as Duke of Passmore.

But on that road lay trouble. He had just begun a descent into dissipation when Julian Everdon, later his sister's husband, plucked him out of London and took him to Somerset to learn how to manage an estate. He was proud of what he'd learned and longed to prove that he could do it on his own. Once again, Julian had given him this opportunity.

Ultimately, the duke had not objected to his sojourn in Somerset. But Geoffrey was not certain his father would countenance his son working as a land steward. Moreover, he did not want to come to

Devonshire as Geoffrey Dorrington, Earl of Cheriton. That would only interfere with his work. So he had contracted the family name and arrived as Geoffrey Dorton, fairly certain that he would not be recognized so far from London.

Geoffrey had not counted on the complications that might arise from such a masquerade. He never expected that here, in north Devonshire, he would find a girl—a lady—who touched him so. And a lady with whom it was impossible to think of a future. His father might very well turn a blind eye to the Earl of Cheriton learning how to run an estate. Indeed, he might approve. But he would never, *never* accept the daughter of an impecunious vicar as the future Duchess of Passmore. No. Geoffrey's duty lay in a marriage of advantage to a daughter of the *ton*.

Clucking his tongue, Geoffrey gently urged his horse forward. As he turned toward the tenant farms, his thoughts remained at the vicarage. His disguise made him seem an acceptable match for a parson's daughter. If Cassie Hartwell found him half as appealing as he found her, she would have every reason to expect a courtship. It was an expectation he could not meet. There must be some way to depress her expectations, but he was quite sure that kissing her was not the way to begin.

Was it one o'clock already? Rodney Gilbert's curricle stood in front of the vicarage and Mrs. Hartwell was scurrying through the house as though the Prince Regent would arrive at any minute.

"Are you dressed, Cassie?" Mrs. Hartwell stood at the foot of the stairs and tried not to shout.

"I am." Cassie descended the front hall, reluctance in every footfall.

"Are you wearing that?" Mrs. Hartwell's face wrinkled in disapproval.

"As you see, Mama."

"You have a perfectly lovely sprigged muslin that has barely been worn. And I'm sure Mr. Gilbert has not seen you in it. That . . . that . . ." Mrs. Hartwell gestured at Cassie's serviceable, brown round gown. "That thing you wear all the time. What will Mr. Gilbert think?"

"I don't care what he thinks." Cassie fetched a loosely woven shawl from the pegs by the kitchen door. "However, he may think that I am a practical woman who would not be so silly as to wear white muslin in which to meet dogs."

"Dogs!" Mrs. Hartwell threw up her hands. "No one *meets* dogs. Mr. Gilbert is taking you to *see* his dogs, and I can assure you, it is not because he wants to introduce you to them. Now . . ." She took the shawl from Cassie and rearranged it around her shoulders. "Go and do yourself some good."

"Yes, Mama." Cassie was quite sure that her definition of "good" differed significantly from her mother's. "But I cannot like that Mr. Gilbert has brought his curricle. There is no room for a chaperone. And I intended to take Dora."

"Dora is needed in the kitchen." Mrs. Hartwell moved toward the door just as the knocker sounded. "And besides, you may drive out in an open carriage without a chaperone. It is not as if Mr. Gilbert is a stranger."

"Yes, Mama." Cassie reached up and gave her tall, spare mother an affectionate kiss.

Within minutes, Mr. Gilbert's curricle was wheeling back toward Gilbert Grange.

"Tell me about your dogs, Mr. Gilbert." Cassie was determined to be as polite as possible and to keep Mr. Gilbert's attention on the purpose of the outing.

"My dogs?" Rodney Gilbert allowed the reins to slacken, and his horse slowed to a sedate trot. Cassie thought that it was probable he could not hold two thoughts in his head at once.

"Yes. Your dogs. The ones we are going to see."

"Hounds." Gilbert picked up the ribbons and resumed a faster pace. "Hunting, don't you know? Do you hunt?"

"Not at all. I barely ride. Our only horses are for the farm, you know." Cassie hoped this little reminder of her reduced circumstances might diminish any interest Rodney Gilbert had in her.

"Oh, naturally, naturally." Gilbert didn't even glance her way and Cassie couldn't tell whether he had actually heard her or whether driving required all of his concentration.

As they drove down Oakleigh High Street, Cassie found herself looking around for a familiar blond head. She was aware that she should not be trying to find Geoffrey Dorton; in fact, she should be avoiding him. But there was a profound sense of disappointment when the only blond head she found belonged to the plumes on Mrs. Pilchard's ridiculously overdone bonnet.

As the curricle crossed the stone bridge over the Tavy and turned into the lane that led to Gilbert Grange, Rodney Gilbert resumed talking about his dogs.

"Brought the whole pack down from Surrey. I bought them at a bargain from an old man whose hunting days were over. Lucky thing Uncle had the empty kennels. Wanted to buy the horses, too, but didn't have the ready. When the Grange is mine,

I'll have some fine hunters. And I'll see that you're mounted and learn to ride."

"Surely Sir Edmund is in good health." Cassie did not care to even think about Rodney Gilbert giving her a horse and teaching her to ride.

"Oh, Uncle's right as rain, but you never know what might happen." Mr. Gilbert's expectant leer sent a chill up Cassie's spine.

The hounds were out of the kennel and milling around a penned area, baying at the top of their lungs. Cassie jumped out of the curricle before Mr. Gilbert could come around to help her and headed immediately for the pen. "What fine animals."

Several of the dogs broke away from the pack and came trotting over to nose Cassie's hand through the fence. She squatted down and began speaking softly to the animals. Soon most of the pack had joined their fellows and were jostling each other to get close to Cassie.

"See here." Rodney Gilbert came up beside Cassie and, wrapping his fingers around her upper arm, dragged her to her feet. "What's all this?"

"I was meeting your dogs. Is that not why you brought me here?"

"Meeting them?" Cassie could see that Mr. Gilbert was baffled by the idea.

"I brought you here to show them to you. You don't meet dogs and you don't talk to them like that. What if they come to expect it? Can't get a good run from a hound that's been coddled." Mr. Gilbert was working himself up into a good choler.

Cassie disengaged her arm from Mr. Gilbert's hand and stepped back from the pen. "I have been here for less than five minutes," she said. "That is hardly sufficient time to begin coddling your dogs."

"Hounds," Mr. Gilbert said.

The moment the dogs realized that Cassie was no longer at the pen, they set up a loud baying and began pushing against the fence.

"Who cares for these dogs?" Cassie asked over the din.

"Don't know. One of my uncle's stable hands, I dare say."

"How long have they been here?" Hands on her hips, Cassie faced Rodney Gilbert.

The man shrank back and shrugged. "Two or three days."

"And you do not know who is caring for them? Do you know if *anyone* is caring for them?" Cassie knew she sounded enraged, and at that moment, she hoped she did.

"They're my hounds." Gilbert's jaw jutted out at a stubborn angle Cassie remembered well from her youth. He always got that expression when he was in the wrong.

"A shame," Cassie said and, turning on her heel, marched out of the stable yard.

"Wait a minute. Where are you going?"

"Home." Cassie kept walking.

"Hold up. I'll get the curricle." Gilbert's voice was an unpleasant mixture of pleading and belligerence.

"I thank you, no. I would rather walk."

After a moment's silence, the baying of the hounds increased, punctuated by a series of sharp yips. Cassie's shoulders tightened at the sound, but she did not turn around. She knew what she would see and there was nothing she could do about it. Right now.

Cassie had not gone a quarter of a mile before Rodney Gilbert's curricle pulled up beside her. "Get in."

Cassie moved closer to the verge and said nothing,

hoping he would just give up and go away, leave Gilbert Grange, leave Oakleigh, leave her alone.

"I am sorry, Miss Hartwell."

Cassie stopped. She didn't turn around. She didn't speak, but it wasn't in her to reject an apology. She waited.

"I should not have spoken to you as I did. It was unforgivable, but I pray you will forgive me."

Still Cassie didn't speak, nor did she look back at Mr. Gilbert, but something in her knew he was casting around for the reason she had left. How could he? How could he not know that she would not tolerate mistreatment of his animals? She nearly felt sorry for his inability to understand.

"And I'm sorry that I did not know who was taking care of the dogs." The poor man sounded so relieved to have hit upon another apology that Cassie unbent enough to allow him to take her back up in his curricle and drive her home.

Chapter 7

Supper was interminable. The boys had eaten earlier in the schoolroom and were in the garden with their books declining verbs. Cassie always preferred to have the boarders at table, as they made the meal lively and distracted her mother from the continuous affront of an unmarried daughter.

"Tell us all about your visit to Gilbert Grange." Mrs. Hartwell had been asking this question in a variety of ways since the meal began. Mr. Hartwell said nothing. Cassie suspected that his mind was in the garden with the boys, looking over their Latin.

"It was short." Cassie forked up a bit of fish pie and chewed with vigor, hoping to forestall any further questions.

Her mother was not to be deterred. "Why was that, dearest?"

Cassie glanced at her father, who had joined the conversation only long enough to give her a vague smile. "We went to see Mr. Gilbert's dogs. We saw the dogs. He returned me to the vicarage."

"Is that all?" Mrs. Hartwell's forehead creased in consternation.

"What more would you like to have happened?" Cassie immediately regretted this question. She knew, only too well, what her mother would have liked.

"Do not pretend to misunderstand me, missy." Mrs. Hartwell set her fork on her plate with a decided click and looked up the table to her husband. "Do you hear her, Mr. Hartwell? Cassie is in the way of making a very advantageous match and will not lift a finger to help herself."

Mr. Hartwell wrinkled his brow. "Is someone courting our Cassie?"

"Mama, please." Cassie flashed an impatient glare at her mother.

"I have hopes for Mr. Gilbert." Mrs. Hartwell shrugged off Cassie's plea.

"That would be very nice." Mr. Hartwell still looked puzzled. He was not in the habit of delving too deeply into his wife's management of the household and family.

"That would *not* be nice, Papa. I cannot like Mr. Gilbert and I certainly do not think that a dance and a curricle ride amount to a courtship."

"Well, they might, my dear. And you don't know Mr. Gilbert well enough to know if you will like him. Give him the opportunity."

Cassie returned her attention to the dish of fish pie in front of her. It never helped to argue with her mother, especially when Mama had a notion to marry off a daughter. Cassie would bide her time and manage this affair herself.

Supper continued in silence until Dora came to remove the dishes and bring in the pudding.

"Have you seen Mr. Dorton?" Mr. Hartwell's question hung in the air above the table, a manifestation of the direction in which both women's thoughts had turned.

"What has he to do with anything?"

Mr. Hartwell blinked at his wife's snappish tone. Cassie sat motionless, wondering where this question had come from and where the discussion would go.

"Eh? Just thought I'd talk to the man about estate management." Mr. Hartwell spooned up some of his lemon custard and lapsed back into silence.

Cassie applied herself to the custard, trying very hard to keep from asking her father what he meant.

As it turned out, it was not necessary. Mrs. Hartwell was never one to let a statement pass without an argument.

"Estate management? Whatever do you need that for? You do well enough with the glebe."

"No, no. For the boys." Mr. Hartwell gestured toward the back garden, where Cassie could hear his students arguing about a verb. "I cannot convince them of the importance of learning their sums. I think they should be shown some practical uses."

"But surely someone else would do just as well." Mrs. Hartwell brightened. "Why not Mr. Gilbert?"

The vicar considered this for a moment and then shook his head. "Young Gilbert has no experience. And the running of Bradworth's more apt to impress young boys. No. It must be Dorton. Cassie, arrange a time, will you?"

Cassie's spoon clattered into her dish and her mother turned to glare at her.

"There is no need to involve Cassie, my dear. Surely you need only send a letter to Bradworth." Mrs. Hartwell peered down the table.

"Hmm. . . . Well, perhaps." The vicar returned to his pudding.

* * *

Cassie gripped the reins of the little cart and wondered, not for the first time, how she had come to be the sole escort for her father's pupils' outing to Bradworth.

Reverend Hartwell had, indeed, written his own note to Mr. Dorton and had, in return, received a graciously worded invitation to bring his charges to the estate offices on Tuesday. The boys had been all agog ever since learning of their impending visit. Even now, Cassie could hear their excited whispers from the back of the cart.

". . . over five thousand acres."

"I heard he mended Ned Towson's roof without being asked."

"I heard he's sweet on Ginny Crocker."

"Gentlemen." Cassie raised her voice to be heard over the steady clip of the pony's hooves. "It is impolite to gossip about your host."

The boys lapsed into abashed silence. Cassie tried to concentrate on the uneven road leading out of the center of Oakleigh, but her thoughts insisted on returning to the very gossip she had just cut short.

It came as no surprise to her that Mr. Dorton had immediately set about repairing the Bradworth tenant cottages. It was just the sort of thing she expected of him. He was probably also kind to his dogs. If he had dogs. Cassie did not imagine he had time to hunt. Or, she reminded herself, the wherewithal. He was a man of no fortune, dependent on his abilities to make his way in the world. She found that vastly appealing.

But Ginny Crocker? Her father, Tom, ran the Bradworth home farm, as well as the largest tenant farm on the estate, and did very well both for himself and his landlord. Ginny was young and pretty. She worked with her mother in the dairy and kept the poultry. She would, undoubtedly, be an ideal wife for a land steward.

Cassie balked at the image of Geoffrey Dorton wed to Ginny Crocker. Was that her mind at work or her heart? Impatient with her own maunderings, Cassie snapped the reins and entered the Bradworth stable yard at a trot.

Geoffrey had carefully prepared for Reverend Hartwell's students. He wanted to show them some of the workings of the estate and then explain how understanding the accounts enabled him to keep everything running smoothly. He was looking forward to becoming better acquainted with the erudite Mr. Hartwell.

When Geoffrey opened the door into the back courtyard, he was surprised to see Miss Cassie Hartwell pulling a dog-cart to a halt in front of his offices. He hurried to greet it.

As Geoffrey helped Miss Hartwell from the hard seat of the cart, he fought to remind himself that she was not someone in whom he should be interested. But Lord, she looked adorable, her bonnet askew over those perpetually tousled chestnut curls and her light frock molded to her rounded little body by the early summer breeze. It was all he could do to release her once she set foot on solid ground.

Geoffrey only had time to give Miss Hartwell an interrogatory look before the three boys tumbled out of the back of the cart and surrounded him, clamoring to know what they would be doing.

"Father has not finished Sunday's sermon," she said in answer to his unasked question. "I have been delegated."

"I find myself delighted." Geoffrey had to admit

that his delight was real. Although he had avoided Cassie Hartwell since Sir Edmund's ball, since he had kissed her and run off into the night, he could not pretend that she had not been on his mind, that he had not watched for her whenever he left the estate. He looked down into her sunny face and could only think about kissing her again. Oh, he was in deep trouble.

"I could have sworn you were avoiding me." Cassie smiled up into his face, her green eyes alight.

Geoffrey stood frozen in that green gaze, unable to respond in any coherent fashion. Yes, he had been avoiding her. Yes, he should still be avoiding her. But at that moment, he could not think of one good reason to do so.

A small hand tapped Geoffrey's arm. "Mr. Dorton, sir. Will you show us the stables? Does Lord Marchbourn have prime horseflesh?"

The boys. Geoffrey tore himself away from his contemplation of Cassie Hartwell's fine eyes and turned his attention to the task at hand.

"Will you introduce me to your companions, Miss Hartwell?" Geoffrey asked, eliciting a grateful smile and the requested introductions.

"Lord Marchbourn does not keep his horses here." Once the introductions were made, Geoffrey answered the boy's question. "But he takes excellent care of the farm horses, which I will show you, as well as a field that is being planted and one of our flocks of sheep. Should you like that?"

"That would be capital, sir." The tallest boy, who had obviously made himself spokesman, spoke formally and politely. Geoffrey flashed Cassie a look that he hoped communicated his appreciation of her father's pupils.

"Would you like to wait in the house, Miss

Hartwell?" Although he could see the sturdy boots peeking out from beneath Miss Hartwell's muslin skirt, Geoffrey did not want her to feel that she must accompany the students as they tramped through the barns and fields.

"Certainly not. I have come to be enlightened as well as the boys." Cassie straightened her straw bonnet and fetched a basket from the back of the cart. "And I have come prepared with refreshment."

Happier than he should be at the notion of a morning with Cassie Hartwell, Geoffrey took the basket and gestured toward the stable. "Let us start here."

The morning was delightful. The spring sun was mitigated by a cool breeze as the troop tramped through the barns, admired the sheep, and asked intelligent questions about how Geoffrey decided what crops to sow. Later, the boys endured a session with the account books. Only the smallest boy seemed truly interested in the accounts and surprised Geoffrey by pointing out an error in one of the totals.

The best part of the day, however, had been walking the fields of Bradworth with Cassie Hartwell at his side. Despite his best intentions, Geoffrey could not help but imagine himself strolling the grounds of his own estate with Cassie beside him. More than once, Geoffrey had to remind himself of Miss Hartwell's unsuitability as a wife. It was impossible. Daughters of vicars did not become duchesses. They married other vicars or farmers or squires.

Geoffrey knew that Rodney Gilbert was courting Cassie Hartwell, and he knew that Mrs. Hartwell encouraged the suit. Surely that was an appropriate pairing. The vicar's daughter and the squire's nephew? Was that not what he thought should happen? Why, then, did the very idea make him wince? Why did the notion of Cassie Gilbert set up such an unholy clamoring in his chest?

"Will you be at the fair, Mr. Dorton?" One of the children looked up from the ledger, his expression expectant.

"Course he will," the oldest boy announced. "Everybody goes to the fair."

"The fair?" Geoffrey raised his head to look at Cassie.

"I forgot that you haven't been here long and don't know about our tradition." Cassie had been sitting to one side of Geoffrey's desk watching him as he explained the accounts to the boys.

"Very true." It hardly seemed possible that he had been in Devonshire only a little over a month. He felt as though he had known Cassie Hartwell all his life.

"Next Sunday, we have to move the stone." Cassie's grin plainly said that she realized he had no idea what she was talking about.

Geoffrey waited for the explanation.

"Local legend has it that the Devil's Stone must be moved every year or Oakleigh will suffer ill luck. May fifteenth is the day all the men in the village gather to move the stone. And, of course, if we're all gathered, we certainly must have a fête."

"The Devil's Stone?" Geoffrey tried to imagine what this might be.

"Yes, that big monolith in the churchyard. They say the devil dropped it in his descent to Hades. We've turned it every year within the memory of everyone in Oakleigh. And this year will be the same."

Geoffrey suddenly remembered the stone she was talking about. It was huge. "But that thing must weigh a hundred stone."

"Very likely. That's why every able-bodied man in Oakleigh takes part. Of course, you'll want to be there." Miss Hartwell cocked an eyebrow at him, her amusement apparent.

Of course he would.

Chapter 8

Cassie rolled onto her side and drew the sheet over her head. She had neglected to close the curtains last night, and the morning sun flooded her room. What time was it?

As if summoned by the thought, her mother cracked open the door and stuck her head into the room. "Still abed, miss?"

"What time is it?"

"Did you not hear the clock strike seven?" Mrs. Hartwell entered the room and pulled the door shut behind her.

"Seven?" Cassie groaned and pulled a pillow over her face.

"It's Fair Day; there's much to do. Now get up and dress yourself. Mr. Gilbert will call for you at noon."

"Call for me?" Casting aside the pillow, Cassie sat up in bed and looked out her window toward the churchyard where tents were already being erected.

"Yes. He asked my permission to escort you to the fair."

Cassie could well imagine the lures her mother had thrown out to elicit that invitation.

"Mama." Cassie gestured toward the window.

"Surely it has not escaped your notice that we are right in the middle of the fair."

Mrs. Hartwell sniffed. Cassie could see she did not intend to give countenance to such a silly notion. Slipping out of bed, Cassie wrapped herself in the ugly woolen shawl she kept at hand for cold nights and early mornings.

Her mother crossed the room and opened the ancient clothespress that had stood against the room's north wall as long as Cassie could remember. Mrs. Hartwell pulled out Cassie's best day dress and gave it a vigorous shake.

As she held it up to the light, Cassie could see that it was starting to wear in places, most particularly where it rubbed against the buckram in her stays. Nevertheless, it was her favorite dress. She thought the creamy muslin and brown sprig brought out the green of her eyes and drew attention away from her unruly hair and complexion that announced the number of hours she spent out of doors.

"This will have to do." Mrs. Hartwell held out the dress. "Put it on before I go down and I'll fasten it for you."

As Cassie struggled to get her hair under control, her thoughts strayed to the day ahead. Why, oh why, had her mother committed her to Rodney Gilbert for the day? She ground her teeth in frustration. Until this morning, her imaginings of the day included attending the fair in the company of Mr. Dorton. But, of course, Mr. Dorton had said nothing to make her think he would even attend, let alone act as her escort.

Foolish girl. Cassie selected a ribbon to match the one trimming her gown and wound it through her hair. What was it about Geoffrey Dorton that created havoc with Cassie's calm, methodical plan for her future? No one else had ever made her want something besides the peaceful home with her parents that she had always envisioned. And what good did such daydreaming accomplish when Geoffrey Dorton had exhibited no interest in the plump daughter of a country parson?

Cassie's fingers, done tying her ribbon, flew to her lips. Perhaps he had exhibited some interest. There was no other explanation for the sudden kiss on Sir Edmund's terrace. But . . . that must have been an aberration, the impulsive gesture of a young man caught up in the romance of a ball.

Even as she tried to convince herself that Geoffrey's kiss meant nothing in light of his later polite indifference, Cassie could not but wonder at what he had meant. Nor could she help wondering at her own powerful reaction.

Oakleigh's May Fair had grown up around the absurd tradition of moving the Devil's Stone every May. What had once been a group of able-bodied men shoving a huge rock into a new position was now a welcome respite from the chores of spring planting. For one day, everyone in the environs gathered to eat, play games, buy goods from the tinkers who flocked to the fair, and cheer on their men as they warded off bad luck for another year. Geoffrey would not have missed it for the world.

The Devil's Stone stood sentinel at the edge of the churchyard, marking the boundary between the cemetery and the common on which the festival was held. In the background squatted the little Saxon church of St. Nectan, untended until the moving of the stone, when the bell would be rung to signal the men to gather.

It was a cloudless day and the early summer sun filtered through the ancient trees surrounding the
common. Geoffrey stood in the shade of a giant yew
and observed the activity. He watched the children
running through the booths, amazed at the number
of them in Oakleigh, and pleased that he was able to
identify Mr. Hartwell's three students, all standing in
rapt attention around a pen of spring lambs.

Then, with an unerring sense, Geoffrey's gaze
moved on. He should have been surprised that he
was able to find Cassie Hartwell so easily among the
people milling around Oakleigh Common. He was
not. Although he had no intention of pursuing
Miss Hartwell, he had given up trying to convince
himself she was not the most appealing woman he
had ever met.

As Geoffrey watched, Miss Hartwell moved easily
among the crowd, stopping to speak to the farmers
and their wives, stooping low to greet the children
clinging to their mothers' skirts.

An old woman emerged from the crowd clutching
a squirming pug to her bosom. The moment the
dog laid eyes on Cassie, it wriggled out of its mistress's arms and bounded up to where Cassie stood
contemplating a selection of preserves. Geoffrey
grinned. That must be Miss Babson and surely that
was Georgie.

Cassie stopped her inspection and sank to the
ground to greet the excited dog. Geoffrey could
hear her soft voice from where he stood. "Hello,
Georgie. Have you come to enjoy the festivities?"

"What is this?" Another voice cut through the din
and a pair of highly shined boots cut off Geoffrey's
view of Miss Hartwell's smiling face.

Gilbert. Geoffrey stiffened. He could not like the

man, and he liked him even less when he was hovering around Miss Hartwell.

Cassie looked up from her conversation with the pug. "I was just talking to Georgie."

"Whose animal is that?" Mr. Gilbert looked repulsed.

"Oh, he's mine, sir." Miss Babson hurried up to reclaim her dog. "I hope he wasn't bothering you, Miss Cassie."

"Of course he wasn't." She gave Georgie a final pat. "We're old friends."

"Come away, Miss Hartwell." Rodney Gilbert took Cassie's arm.

Geoffrey took a step forward, ready to intervene, before he caught himself. Mr. Gilbert was probably her escort. Geoffrey had no business interfering in Cassie Hartwell's personal life. He sighed and forced himself to turn away.

Cassie cringed at Rodney Gilbert's touch. It took a great deal of concentration not to pull away from him. But she had promised her mother that she would attend with Rodney, and there was nothing to be done but grit her teeth and get through the day.

She thought she had seen Mr. Dorton on the edge of the crowd earlier, but when she looked back he was gone. She peered into the crowd.

"I wish you would not grovel in the dirt with dogs."

In her search for Geoffrey Dorton, Cassie had managed, for a moment, to forget her escort. "I beg your pardon?" She might have allowed Mr. Gilbert's escort today, but she had definitely not given him leave to address her actions.

"Your father is a gentleman, Miss Hartwell. You should behave like a gentleman's daughter."

Cassie pulled her arm from Mr. Gilbert's grasp and moved around to face him. "I gave you no leave to comment on my behavior."

Mr. Gilbert smiled and a chill chased down Cassie's spine. "I flatter myself that I might soon have the pleasure of doing so."

"Flatter yourself all you like, Mr. Gilbert, but never tell me how to act again." Cassie stomped off toward the sheep pen.

By the time Mr. Gilbert caught up with her, Cassie had managed to subdue her rage.

"My apologies, Miss Hartwell. I obviously overstepped the bounds."

"Obviously." Cassie was not quite ready to be charitable.

"I hope you will not let my unfortunate remark ruin the rest of the day. I would very much like to see the rest of the festival with you." Mr. Gilbert looked appropriately repentant.

Remembering her promise to her mother, Cassie nodded once and placed her hand on Mr. Gilbert's offered arm. This, she promised herself, was the last time.

It was not horrible. Mr. Gilbert went out of his way to be solicitous and refrained from any more comments on her conduct. The day continued mild, and Cassie had ample opportunity to talk to her neighbors and play with the children. She stopped to buy a light luncheon and examine the wares spread out on the grass in front of a caravan.

Just as Cassie had bitten into a savory meat pie, the church bell rang once. It was time to move the Devil's Stone. Cassie wiped her chin with her handkerchief and moved toward the monolith, Mr. Gilbert in her wake.

Most of the able-bodied men in the village were

gathered in front of the stone discussing their strategy. Cassie glanced at her escort. "Are you not going to help move the stone?"

Mr. Gilbert looked shocked at the suggestion. "Certainly not. No gentleman would."

Cassie looked back at the group of men. She had to admit that they all looked as though they engaged in manual labor. But she had been in Oakleigh all her life and knew the traditions.

"Every man who can, does," she said. "When my father was younger, he helped move the stone. Why, I even remember Lord Bradworth helping to move it when I was a girl."

"Well, they're not moving it now. And I don't intend to dirty my hands alongside common laborers." Mr. Gilbert tugged at the sleeves of his fastidiously tailored jacket.

"Mr. Dorton is among them." Cassie looked back at the knot of men. Mr. Dorton was not only among them, he was the magnetic center of the group. Like a lodestone, Cassie's gaze kept returning to him. Like the rest of the men, he had removed his jacket and rolled up his sleeves, revealing broad, muscular shoulders and forearms corded by hard work and burnished by the sun. He took her breath away.

Rodney Gilbert snorted. "Dorton is no gentleman. Look at him. No gentleman would allow himself to become so tanned and work hardened."

Cassie stiffened.

"Oh, I dare say, he would attract enough attention in London," Gilbert continued. "He's probably quite the rake when he's in town. No doubt, he'll snag himself the daughter of some cit with a fortune and set himself up as a gentleman. But Dorton a true gentleman? I think not."

Chapter 9

"Great heavens! Do you really do this every year?"
Geoffrey leaned over with his hands on his knees,
trying to stop his arms from trembling. Around
him, farmers from the Bradworth Estate gathered
in a circle and, by turn, patted his shoulder or in-
dulged in some good-humored joking.

Finally, Tom Crocker spoke. "Aye, we do it every
year and have yet to have a bad harvest or a rash o'
illness. Now you're one o' us, I expect you'll do it
every year yerself."

Geoffrey straightened and smiled. He *was* one of
them. Nearly crippling himself as he and the rest of
Oakleigh's men wrestled the great rock into a new
position had made him one of them as no other act
could have done.

"Well done, gentlemen." The soft voice could be-
long to no one else. Geoffrey looked over to see
Cassie Hartwell and two other women approaching
with a foaming pitcher and trays full of mugs.

The men laughed and fell on the ale as soon as it
had been set down on a nearby table. "The best
part of the fair," one said as he accepted a brimming glass from Miss Hartwell. "That first swallow
after the rock is moved." He suited action to words

and then wiped his mouth with the back of his hand, grinning all the while.

Geoffrey took a deep draught from his own mug and looked up into the smiling eyes of Cassie Hartwell. Immediately, he was aware of the inappropriate state of his attire. Even surrounded by a score of men in their shirtsleeves, he felt exposed. Quickly, he rolled down his own sleeves and retrieved his jacket from the branch on which he had hung it. There was nothing for his cravat but to shove it into a pocket.

"Where is your escort, Miss Hartwell?" The moment the words were out of his mouth, Geoffrey wished them unsaid. They evinced too acute an awareness of Cassie Hartwell's activity that day.

Rolling her eyes, Miss Hartwell responded without the least self-consciousness. "Mr. Gilbert has been lured away to observe the racing. I believe he has a wager on one of his uncle's horses." She did not look the least displeased by the loss of her companion.

"Perhaps I might prove an acceptable substitute." Despite every good intention, Geoffrey could not stop himself from making the offer.

Cassie colored and Geoffrey felt absurdly gratified that his invitation should provoke such a response.

"I would be delighted to have your company." Cassie slipped her hand into the crook of Geoffrey's arm and cocked her head at him expectantly.

The crowd was beginning to thin and some of the farmers were packing up their wares and preparing to go home. But all was not over. There would be a bonfire tonight before everyone returned to their work. In the meantime, there was the race and some contests for the children. There was still food and drink and the lovely shade of the wood on the far side of the common for a secluded walk.

Geoffrey tamped down an almost overwhelming desire to whisk Cassie into the wood. "Some lemonade?" He nodded toward the table where the beverage was still being dispensed.

"Of course."

Did disappointment flash across Miss Hartwell's mobile features? This was not going at all well. Geoffrey was torn between an insistent craving for Cassie Hartwell's company and the sure knowledge that he should not be seeking it.

"And then perhaps a stroll." At the moment, the craving seemed to be winning out.

Geoffrey picked up the mugs of lemonade and motioned toward the edge of the common where two of the upturned logs that served as makeshift seating stood empty. They sat in companionable silence for several minutes, sipping their drinks and watching a footrace among the young boys, until the unmistakable odor of fish signaled that they were about to have company.

"Brummell." Miss Hartwell, as always, sounded delighted to see the huge dog.

Brummell, however, was beside himself to see Geoffrey. With barely a nod to his champion, he sidled up to Geoffrey and peered into his mug.

"This is not for you," Geoffrey told him.

The dog huffed and sat down, leaning heavily against Geoffrey's doeskin-clad leg.

Geoffrey glanced at his companion. "I don't know why he has chosen me."

Cassie gave him an amused grin and a shake of her head. "He's a dog. He has unerring instincts about people."

That assessment warmed Geoffrey to his toes. He reached out to scratch the smelly dog behind his ears. Brummell groaned in appreciation and threw himself to the ground, where he put his head on Geoffrey's boot and promptly began to snore.

"Have you been a steward long?"

Geoffrey's previously warmed heart sank. This was why he could not court Cassie Hartwell. The truth of his position made an alliance impossible and now he had to lie to her.

"A while," he said in as neutral a tone as possible. "I worked for my sister's husband to learn the occupation and then Lord Marchbourn offered me this position." There. That was the truth, if not all of it.

"Then your sister's husband is a land steward as well?" Cassie looked interested in the subject and oblivious of the havoc she was creating within Geoffrey's conscience.

"He . . . he runs an estate. Yes." Geoffrey shifted on this seat.

"I envy you your occupation." Cassie turned a gentle smile toward Geoffrey, and he knew, in his heart, how she felt. He had felt exactly the same way when he had thought there was no alternative to spending his days in idle dissipation.

Without thinking, Geoffrey took Miss Hartwell's hand in his. "It is a blessing," he said, looking down at their linked hands.

When Geoffrey raised his head to find Cassie blushing, he immediately realized what he had done and released her hand.

"Tell me about your family," he said, trying to cover his confusion.

Cassie, still blushing, looked away for a moment, drawing in a deep breath and straightening her shoulders. As she began to speak, she continued to look out onto the green.

"You know Mama and Papa," she said.

"Yes, but that is all I know. Have you always been in Oakleigh?"

"Yes. I was born here, as were my sisters. Lord Bradworth offered my father the living right after he finished his studies. So this has always been our home. And I hope it always will be." She finally turned to look at Geoffrey.

"Do you, indeed?" Geoffrey pretended not to understand why this statement made him unhappy. "I would have thought you might be interested in travel."

Cassie laughed. "I try very hard not to interest myself in those things I cannot have."

It was Geoffrey's turn to redden. It had been terribly rude to bring up the subject when it should have been apparent that the daughter of a country vicar would not have the means to follow any of her dreams. He cast about for a safer avenue of conversation.

"I like your name," he said, finally. "Is your mother's name Cassandra as well?"

Miss Hartwell put her hands over her mouth and giggled, a sound Geoffrey had previously discovered to be one of his very favorite sounds in the world.

"I assume that means it is not," he said, enjoying her continued laughter.

"I am the youngest of eight daughters," Cassie said when she stopped laughing. "Did you know that?"

Geoffrey shook his head. "I thought you were the only child."

"I have seven lovely sisters." Cassie stopped for a moment, shrugged, and went on. "Well, six lovely sisters and . . . another. They're all quite contentedly married and off with their husbands and children. Some quite far away."

Geoffrey was not sure where this was going, but was happy to wait in silence to find out.

"I think my mother must have known that I would be her last child." Cassie's mouth quirked as she suppressed another laugh. "My full name is Caspar Whittley Maria Hartwell," she managed to say before bursting into giggles once more.

Geoffrey snorted.

"Precisely," Cassie gasped between giggles. "Precisely the correct response."

"May I ask why you are named Caspar Whittley Maria Hartwell?" Geoffrey was having difficulty not succumbing to his own fit of laughter.

"My great-uncle," Cassie said, her giggles subsiding a bit. "Caspar Whittley, Viscount Reading. Actually, my grandmother's cousin. My dear mother held out hope until the bitter end—that would be me—that she would have a son who would garner Uncle Whittley's attention and bring us all into fashion."

"Oh my." Geoffrey stopped chuckling. "Was that so important to your mother?"

"It was." Cassie's laughter had stopped as well. "It probably still is. She has never forgotten that her mother was the cousin of a viscount. It's the reason she is throwing me at Rodney Gilbert's head—oh dear." Cassie clapped a hand over her mouth. "I shouldn't have said that."

"Never mind." Geoffrey reached for his mug.

Cassie picked up her lemonade and emptied it in one long, thirsty swallow. Unable to turn away, Geoffrey watched, fascinated, as her tongue crept out to capture the last drops of the tart liquid from her rosy lips. He clutched his own untouched drink in his hand.

"Well?" Cassie's bright glance caught his. "What shall we do now?"

There was nothing for it. Geoffrey had to taste the lemonade on those soft lips. "A . . . er . . . stroll perhaps?" He glanced toward the wood.

"Oh yes." Cassie fairly glowed at the suggestion, and Geoffrey's heart performed a jig before faltering in the face of what he was about to do.

It was only a short distance to the edge of the common where the trees grew closer together and provided a screen against anyone who might be still at the fair. Just before they entered the nearest path into the wood, Geoffrey stopped and looked down at the young woman on his arm.

"Will not Mr. Gilbert be looking for you?" He wasn't sure what he wanted the answer to be. He should not be taking Miss Caspar Whittley Maria Hartwell into the woods with the intention of kissing her, and he should welcome an excuse not to do so. But, oh, how he longed to have one more taste of those lips.

Cassie hesitated and then shrugged. "I don't care," she said, lightly touching his sleeve.

It was the touch that decided it. Like a spark to tinder, the heat of that feathery contact ignited Geoffrey's blood and quashed every reservation. Putting his hand over hers, he led her into the shady pathway.

They did not walk far. It was not a great distance to the point where they were invisible to anyone observing from the common. Geoffrey only hoped no one had seen them leave. Beside him, Geoffrey could hear Cassie's breathing quicken. She had not misunderstood his intentions.

As they approached an aged oak in the middle of the path, Geoffrey pulled back. He should not be doing this. He had nothing to offer Cassie Hartwell, and he was not brought up to dally with innocent young women. Six feet from the tree, he stopped dead. "We must go back."

"No." Cassie slid her hand down to his and tugged at his arm. "Not yet."

"We shouldn't be here. I don't know what I was thinking. I must get you back."

Before Geoffrey could turn around, one of Cassie's hands had gripped his jacket and the other was on the back of his neck, urging his head toward her.

"Cassie," he groaned and relinquished the fight.

This was not like the last kiss, quick and hard and stolen. This was a kiss of intention. When Geoffrey's lips met hers, they softened and melded, drinking in the tart taste of lemons and the sweetness of Cassie Hartwell. He brought his hands up to her waist and pulled her toward him until the length of her rounded body was flush against his.

The kiss became more urgent. Geoffrey could hear Cassie murmur in the back of her throat, and the sound set him aflame. He slid his hands to her hips and was about to deepen the kiss when her gasp recalled him to where he was and what he was doing.

With an effort that was almost beyond him, Geoffrey moved his hands to Cassie's shoulders and set her away from him. He leaned his forehead against hers and, in a hoarse whisper, asked her forgiveness.

"Never." Cassie's voice was as unsteady as his.

Geoffrey's head jerked up.

"I will not forgive where there is no fault. I wanted that as much as you." Cassie hesitated. "Perhaps more."

As Geoffrey gazed in muddled incomprehension, Cassie smoothed out her dress and straightened her hair. Then, she raised herself on tiptoe and planted a soft kiss on Geoffrey's mouth before turning and running back toward the fair.

Chapter 10

Emerging from the wood, Cassie nearly tripped over Brummell, who was lying in wait right on the grassy verge. The dog bolted upright and woofed inquiringly.

"He's still in there," Cassie said, too bewildered by her own actions to wonder whether the dog understood her.

Brummell woofed again and trotted into the woods at the point where Cassie had exited, leaving little question as to whether he knew what she had said.

Cassie walked carefully to the tree stumps on which she and Geoffrey had sat and looked around. No one seemed to have noticed her exit from the wooded area. She took time now to wonder whether anyone had noticed her entrance. She should have thought of this before wandering off with Geoffrey Dorton.

But she had thought of nothing other than the magnetic presence of the man beside her. Nothing but what it would be like to kiss him again.

Sighing, Cassie sank to one of the rustic stools and picked up the mug that sat on the other. She raised it to her lips. The mug was almost empty, but she had no interest in drinking. Her only interest was in the lips that had just recently touched the rim of the mug and that had, even more recently, touched her own. She sighed again. She was far too fascinated by Geoffrey Dorton. Her mother would have an apoplexy if she knew she had gone with him apart from the crowd and kissed him.

Slowly, Cassie lowered the mug from her lips. Letting it lie loosely in her lap, she considered the kiss. Surely, Geoffrey had taken her into the trees with the intention of kissing her. But, just as surely, she had initiated the kiss. He had gone all gentlemanly on her just moments before she had pulled his head to hers.

She was twenty-seven years old and had been kissed before by one or two of the gentlemen who might have turned out to be suitors had they stayed around. And kissed by one memorable farmer's lad with broad shoulders and sunburnt skin whose lips had tasted like summer. But never had she initiated the kiss and never had she wanted one quite so much. None of the kisses of her girlhood moved her the way Geoffrey Dorton's kiss did.

Geoffrey's kiss had been a paean to tenderness, almost reverent in the way his lips moved over hers, but she had sensed the passion banked beneath the soft supplication. It was a kiss to which one might become addicted.

"There you are."

Cassie started and dropped the mug. Rodney Gilbert loomed over her, his hat in his hand and his face glistening with perspiration. "M—Mr. Gilbert."

A fresh breeze swept through the trees, bringing the scent of oak and ash and the sound of children's voices from a distant place. Cassie turned her head into it, seeking to cool her burning cheeks.

Rodney bent down and picked up the mug. "I looked for you earlier, but you weren't here. One of the boys said he thought you'd gone home." He nodded his head toward a bench on the other side of the common.

Cassie looked toward the bench where her father's students had their heads together, sharing a pasty. Had they seen her leave with Geoffrey? If so, she blessed them for discretion beyond their years.

"I went for a walk." Cassie tried to sound nonchalant, wondering that Mr. Gilbert did not hear the mad racing of her heart.

"Alone?" Mr. Gilbert's sharp tone brought Cassie's head up to stare at him.

"Naturally." Cassie infused her voice with as much disdain as she could muster.

"I thought I saw Dorton sniffing around earlier. I don't want you to associate with him."

"I beg your pardon?" Rodney Gilbert's effrontery left Cassie nearly speechless.

As if Cassie had genuinely not heard him the first time, Gilbert repeated his warning.

Cassie rose to her feet and stalked across the common toward the clearing where some of the village men were just putting the final touches on the bonfire. She had been there less than a minute when Mr. Gilbert came up beside her, his hat in his hand, and touched her arm.

"It seems as though I have put another foot wrong," he said without removing his hand.

Cassie shrugged away. "Yes. So it seems."

"I beg your forgiveness. I was too hasty."

Cassie said nothing.

"Can you not find it in your heart to forgive me this time?"

The wheedling tone set Cassie's teeth on edge,

but she refused to allow Rodney Gilbert to force her to create a scene in a public place.

"I assure you, Mr. Gilbert, that I already have sufficient people looking out for my interests. I will overlook your presumption one more time. But I will not do so again."

This seemed to satisfy Mr. Gilbert. He bowed and replaced his hat. "Allow me to purchase supper before the bonfire is lit."

When Rodney Gilbert returned with the food, he wore a worried look on his face.

"Is something amiss?" Cassie asked as she accepted the pasty from her companion.

"I fear there is an injured animal in the woods. Some of the boys said they saw a dog run into the trees. And I could hear something that sounded like a dog in pain."

Casting aside her pasty, Cassie rose from her seat. "I must find out."

"Of course you must. I'll take you there." Gilbert set down his own food and his tankard of ale.

Away from the fire, the wood was gloomy in the falling dusk. Cassie hesitated at the edge of the clearing and cocked her head. "I hear nothing."

"Oh my. I hope the dog isn't too injured to make any sound." Rodney Gilbert seized her arm and urged her toward the trees.

Cassie bit her lip. This all seemed somewhat spurious. Hesitating, she looked around the clearing. She couldn't see either Brummell or Georgie. And both had been there earlier. She wasn't willing to risk abandoning any injured animal, so she tamped down her suspicions and walked into the wood.

* * *

Geoffrey found himself a friendly log a short distance beyond the oak tree under which he had kissed Cassie Hartwell—or under which she had kissed him. He took a seat and leaned back to look up at the sky, blue as sapphires through the leafy canopy of the woods. He could hear the sounds from the fair like a distant tinkling of bells.

Within minutes, he could also hear the sound of huge paws padding through the undergrowth. Brummell emerged from between two low bushes, trotted over, and flopped down beside him with a contented groan. Geoffrey shook his head. It seemed as though he had himself an admirer.

It seemed as though he had himself more than one. The sensation of Cassie Hartwell's soft lips against his, the pressure of her hand on the back of his neck, the delight of her compact little body pressed against his filtered through his mind, leaving him bemused and thoroughly aroused.

Whatever was he going to do about this? It was one thing to fight his own attraction to Cassie, but he wasn't sure he had the inner resources to fight hers as well. Geoffrey leaned down and scratched Brummell's ears, eliciting a huff of satisfaction, and began enumerating the reasons he could not pursue Cassie Hartwell.

Regardless of his feelings, his desires, or his interests, he would, one day, be a duke. He prayed that the day would be far into the future, and given his father's robust constitution, likely it would be. Nevertheless, there were certain expectations that go with being the heir to a dukedom and Geoffrey had grown up inculcated with every one of them.

The expectations included how he performed at school, what he would do when he left university, how he would conduct himself, where he would live, whom he would marry.

Geoffrey had already disappointed his father more than he cared to remember. Although he had finished school, he had not done so with distinction. And his first season in London after coming down from Oxford had been an embarrassment to both himself and his family.

The duke had put up with quite a lot, and Geoffrey was ready to make him proud to call him his heir. Geoffrey had escaped the embarrassment of his excessive indulgence by taking himself off to learn to be a land steward. In that he hoped to please and impress his father. He could do no less in his choice of bride. Inevitably he would have to return to town and choose one from among the daughters of peers who inhabited his father's circle. And that meant that Cassie Hartwell would not do.

Nor was Geoffrey the kind of man who dallied with innocents and left them to their own devices when he had done with them. Even had the lady in question not been Cassie Hartwell, Geoffrey would have taken care to keep his distance and not raise expectations. The problem seemed to be that Cassie had taken possession of his heart. Now none of it would be easy.

Brummell lurched to his feet, dragging Geoffrey away from his thoughts. The sun had dropped over the horizon, leaving the rosy twilight of a spring evening. The bonfire would be lit soon. Clicking his tongue at the panting dog, Geoffrey strode toward the fairground.

It was full dark by the time the fire was lit. Villagers from Oakleigh and the surrounding farms stood in little groups around the fire, talking and laughing. Maids from the Blue Unicorn served up tankards of ale and the ever-present pasties. A small band was tuning up at the edge of the clearing.

Brummell, spying the man who fed him, ran off, leaving Geoffrey alone at the edge of a group. Without thought, his gaze roamed the crowd. Where was Cassie? Had she gone home after their walk in the woods? If she stayed, she would certainly be among the villagers, who obviously adored her.

"Good evening, Mr. Dorton. Have you seen Cassie?"

"I'm sorry, Reverend Hartwell. I haven't seen her since before sunset." Geoffrey's heart sank. If Mr. Hartwell didn't know where Cassie was, then she hadn't gone home. Where was she?

The vicar's face was screwed up in a perplexed grimace. "Mrs. Hartwell does not seem to be concerned, but it's not like Cassie to disappear without a word."

"Shall I help you look for her?"

Mr. Harwell's expression cleared. "Would you? It's fair dark and my old eyes don't do so well after the sun goes down."

Geoffrey glanced toward the bonfire. He could see couples laughing and dancing, and noticed a few sneaking away into the shadows.

"Why don't you walk around the fire and see if you can find anyone who has s...n Miss Hartwell, and I'll look along the edges of the common?"

Mr. Hartwell grasped Geoffrey's hand in both of his. "I thank you, sir. I truly do appreciate your kindness."

"It is nothing." Geoffrey shook the older man's hand and edged away from the firelight.

Had Rodney Gilbert rejoined Miss Hartwell? The thought caused a sudden plummeting of Geoffrey's heart. He had taken an instant dislike to the squire's nephew. He didn't like his proprietary air around Cassie, and he was quite sure Cassie didn't like it either. It seemed unlikely, then, that she had gone willingly on a moonlit stroll with the man. Especially after that kiss. . . .

Nevertheless, Geoffrey would rule out nothing. Cassie Hartwell was still as much a mystery to him as his own feelings about her.

As Geoffrey strode the perimeter of the fairgrounds, peering into darkened niches in the greenery and listening for the sound of voices and footsteps, Brummell bounded out of the woods and, with a loud woof, put his paws on Geoffrey's shoulders.

Geoffrey pushed him away. "Not now, Brummell. Go home."

The dog jumped again, this time butting Geoffrey's chest with his head.

Geoffrey shoved at the dog and then brought his hands to his chest, aware that he now smelled like day-old haddock.

Brummell made to jump again and Geoffrey raised a hand. "What do you want?"

Almost as if he understood the question, the dog started back to the trees, looking over his shoulder at Geoffrey as he did so.

Sighing in exasperation, Geoffrey followed.

Brummell galloped ahead into the murky darkness of the wood. Geoffrey stumbled after him trying to let his eyes adjust to the diminished light, following the sound of the dog's huge paws on the packed earth.

Ahead, the dog skidded to a halt and Geoffrey could hear voices.

"There is no injured animal here." Cassie Hartwell, without a doubt, and sounding seriously displeased.

"It is my heart that is wounded, Cassie, and only your kiss will heal it."

Good God, was that drivel supposed to be attractive? Geoffrey knew immediately that the insinuating murmur could only be Rodney Gilbert. He squinted into the gloom and could just make out two figures not far from the spot on which he had kissed Cassie Hartwell—or she had kissed him.

Geoffrey hesitated, unsure for a moment whether Cassie would welcome his interference. Her unladylike snort told him everything he needed to know.

He stepped quietly on the path and reached them just as Mr. Gilbert was reaching for Cassie's hand.

"There you are, Miss Hartwell."

Cassie whirled toward him. Geoffrey had come close enough to see both her welcoming smile and Gilbert's irritated snarl.

"You're not welcome here, Dorton." Gilbert stepped forward and attempted to put an arm around Cassie's shoulders.

Cassie immediately moved away and came to stand beside Geoffrey. "Were you looking for me?"

"Your father is worried about you." Without a glance at Gilbert, Geoffrey held out his arm.

Cassie slid her hand around his elbow and blew out a small sigh. "I do not wish to worry Papa," she said.

As they walked away from the oak and from Mr. Gilbert, Brummell romping at their side, Cassie murmured a heartfelt "thank you," and moved a little closer to Geoffrey.

Chapter 11

Cassie had spent a restless night, alternately fuming over Rodney Gilbert's annoyingly possessive behavior and savoring the sweetness of kissing Geoffrey Dorton under the oak tree. When she finally slept, her dreams were lovely. She woke more than once with her night rail twisted around her knees and her head full of Geoffrey.

What was she to do? Both her mother and Mr. Gilbert seemed determined to press her into his company whether or not she desired it. Truth be told, her desires tended solely toward the fair-haired steward who had stolen, unbidden, into her heart.

Morning came with unwelcome promptness and Cassie dragged herself out of bed and over to the window. She stood, staring down into the back garden, scrubbing her hands over her face. It was Tuesday, her day to visit the housebound in Oakleigh parish, bringing food and remedies and a little company to the elderly and infirm among her father's flock. She had gladly assumed this task once she was old enough to carry a basket and wise enough to know who, among the parish, needed what. And her mother had gladly relinquished the task, preferring to stay at home and engage in less tiring activities.

Cassie pulled on her blue-and-white-striped dimity dress and tied the blue sash around the slightly raised waist. The dress was serviceable and still attractive enough to wear making calls. She told herself that it would not do to embarrass her father, but in the back of her mind, she wondered if she would meet Geoffrey Dorton during her travels today.

She did not linger over breakfast, downing a piece of toast and a single cup of tea before going into the kitchen to pack her basket. After checking the parcels and bidding good day to Dora and the cook, Cassie left for the first of her calls.

By noon, she had dispatched most of her visits in Oakleigh proper and returned home for another cup of tea. Her mother joined her in the kitchen as she was refilling her basket.

"What? Not done with your calls?" Mrs. Hartwell peered into the basket and rearranged a few of the packets.

"Tuesdays are always a long day." Cassie continued packing.

"Did Mr. Gilbert offer to accompany you?" Mrs. Hartwell stood back and examined Cassie's handiwork, twitching one last bundle into position.

"No, Mama." Cassie sighed in exasperation.

"Did you tell him about your errands?"

"No, Mama."

"Why ever not? I am certain Mr. Gilbert would have been happy to escort you."

"Are you indeed?" Cassie stopped in the middle of counting loaves of bread to glance up at her mother.

"Do not be pert, miss."

"Do not push me, Mama. I don't wish to spend

any more time with Mr. Gilbert, and I feel sure that he will be relieved to hear it."

"What fustian. He has been most assiduous in his attentions." Mrs. Hartwell folded her arms across her chest in a militant stance.

"I think not." Cassie did not look at her mother as she finished packing her basket. "Mr. Gilbert's attentions have been the result of your own assiduity—and that of Sir Edmund. Left to his own devices, Rodney Gilbert would have nothing to do with me. I assure you, I have seen the last of Mr. Rodney Gilbert." Cassie strode through the door into the back garden to the sound of her mother's tongue clicking in disapproval.

The afternoon calls took Cassie across the fields of several of the village farms. As she climbed over a stile onto Bradworth land, she was struck with a vivid recollection of her first meeting with Geoffrey Dorton in that very field. She smiled to herself at the image of Geoffrey pinned to the ground by an enthusiastically affectionate wolfhound. Cassie reached the ground, shook out her skirts, picked up her basket, and started off, the memory lingering in her mind and the smile on her lips.

Cassie skirted the field, staying close to the low walls and hedges that enclosed the plot to avoid the newly plowed furrows. This route took longer, but Cassie did not hurry, enjoying the warmth of the spring afternoon and the country smells of newly turned earth and budding trees.

She tarried a bit along the hedge separating Bradworth land from that belonging to Gilbert Grange, hoping to run into Bradworth's stalwart steward. When it became apparent that Geoffrey Dorton was not riding this particular field, Cassie hefted her basket and slid through the hedges.

The path brought Cassie uncomfortably close to the Gilbert Grange stable block, but it really was the most direct route to Mrs. Smith, and the elderly widow depended on Cassie's Tuesday call.

As she hurried past the paddock fence in back of the stables, Cassie was arrested by the unmistakable sound of a dog in pain. She hesitated for only a moment before clambering through the fence and stealing around the corner of the building toward the source of the canine yelps.

Rounding the corner into the courtyard, Cassie came to a sudden halt and then crept back into the shadow of the stone stable. Rodney Gilbert stood in the yard outside the kennel, crop in hand and arm upraised. Several of his hounds cowered around the edges of the pen. One stood before him with a terrified look as Gilbert brought the crop down on the dog's back, raising a welt along the white fur and eliciting another howl of pain.

"Insufferable cur." Gilbert raised his hand again and the dog put back his ears and lowered his head, waiting for another blow.

Cassie's first instinct was to cry out herself and then to march into that pen and snatch the crop from Mr. Gilbert's hand. She was just about to act when Gilbert dropped his arm and stalked out of the yard, leaving the dogs huddled in the corner of the pen looking terrified and forlorn.

The beating was over—for now. Cassie slowly moved from her position, reluctant to leave the dogs to the mercies of their owner. But there was nothing she could do now, and Mrs. Smith was expecting her. Cassie edged away from the stable and returned to the path along the fence.

Normally, Cassie tried to keep calls on Mrs. Smith as short as possible. She knew the old woman was lonely and tried not to begrudge her fifteen or twenty minutes of gossip. But she was always ready to be on her way once the widow launched into stories of the old days. Today, Cassie settled into a chair at the rough-hewn table that dominated the widow's single room and allowed the old lady's chatter to wash over her. Mrs. Smith was her last call and she did not mean to leave until the sun was nearly set.

"And then Mr. Smith packed me up and moved me out of that dingy room to Devon." Mrs. Smith's toothless mouth curved into a dreamy smile. "It were like heaven. The green countryside and Mr. Smith to hold my hand on the long nights. If you know what I mean." She gave Cassie a knowing wink.

Cassie sighed. Oh yes. She could imagine what Mrs. Smith meant, could picture herself in the Bradworth steward's cottage, holding out her arms to a dusty Geoffrey just returned from a long day in the fields, could imagine in a vague sort of way the holding that went on during the long nights. Her glance met the widow's in a yearning smile of acknowledgment.

The sun was low, the farm buildings casting long shadows as Cassie crept back toward the Gilbert Grange kennel. She peered around the corner and breathed a sigh of relief. No one seemed to be about. Rummaging in her basket for the wedge of cheese she had held back from her deliveries, Cassie advanced toward the dogs.

Alerted by their sensitive sense of smell, the hounds surged toward the fence as Cassie approached. Fortunately, they identified her as neither foe nor quarry and greeted her only with some low whining.

As quietly as possible, Cassie slipped the latch to the pen and eased inside. The dogs gathered around her, panting anxiously as she distributed a bit of cheese to each. How she wished she could explain to them what was going to happen and ask them to cooperate. Steeling herself, she opened the gate and, signaling to the dogs, hurried back toward the fence.

To Cassie's relief, the pack trotted quietly after her. The long spring twilight had begun as Cassie and her retinue slid through the hedge and started off around the fields. She hoped the lengthening shadows would help conceal her from anyone at the Grange.

Once in the open field, the pack fanned out, noses to the ground, instincts at the fore. Cassie stopped and watched them harry the bushes and snuffle the furrows. If they were determined to hunt, she would never get them to safety.

Suddenly, one of the dogs gave a short bark and the pack came to a standstill. To a dog, they turned their heads and looked at the hound Cassie now identified as the leader. This dog, bless him, left off his investigations and trotted back to Cassie. He sat down in front of her and gazed up with unmistakable intent.

Cassie dropped to her knees and embraced the rough neck. Sitting back, she fingered the hound's silky ears. "Thank you . . . Attila," she whispered, naming the pack leader on the spot. "I promise you won't regret it." The pack reassembled around Attila, and Cassie passed out a few more bits of cheese.

Cassie chuckled as she and her pack continued their trek. Attila's acceptance seemed to have ceded leadership status to her—or perhaps it was the basket, still redolent of good Devonshire cheddar. Whatever the reason, Cassie was now surrounded by gamboling dogs who frequently interrupted their march to bump against her legs or take a quick lick of her hand. They had become quite a merry party.

Cassie was halfway to Bradworth when she realized what she was doing. During her prolonged call on Mrs. Smith, she had planned to return to Gilbert Grange and rescue the dogs. But, at some point in this plan, her usual common sense had fled and she had taken the dogs with no clear idea of what she would do with them.

Only when she crossed the boundary onto Bradworth land with a pack of snuffling hounds at her heels did she realize that her best hope, indeed her only option, was to take them to Geoffrey and ask him to house them. Not for a moment did she doubt that he would.

Cassie was just entering the wooded park in back of Bradworth Hall when a large shadow galloped out of the trees and joined her pack, woofing merrily. The hounds took one look at Brummell and started baying.

"Stop it," Cassie hissed at the big dog who was now romping happily around the pack. "I didn't bring them for you."

Brummell obviously did not believe this Banbury tale. He sidled up to Cassie and, pushing his nose into her palm, woofed again in thanks.

Cassie grasped the fur at the back of Brummell's neck and kept him at her side. Fortunately, the big dog moderated his joy just enough to convince the hounds to leave off their baying and regroup around Cassie and her new escort. Cassie released her hold on the wolfhound, but let her hand rest against his neck. Brummell was content to pad quietly at her side until she emerged from the trees and started up the path toward the rear courtyard.

Once the Bradworth stable was in sight, Brummell bounded off, followed by the hounds. Their noses to the ground, the pack tracked their new leader right to the stable door. Which opened to reveal Jemmy Crocker, newly apprenticed to Bradworth's Clerk of the Stables.

"Miss Cassie." The boy goggled at the pack of hounds who had left Brummell to mill around Cassie's skirts.

"Jemmy." Cassie's glance swept the stable yard. "Can you help me? I need a place to keep these dogs for the night."

Jemmy hesitated. "Mr. Dorton ain't here right now."

"Yes, I see." Cassie wrung her hands as she looked around one more time. "But surely, he won't mind. It's just for tonight."

"Well, since it's you, miss, I suppose he won't." The boy opened the stable door wider and beckoned Cassie and her charges inside.

"I'll wait and speak to him, shall I?" Cassie strode the length of the stable to the enclosure that had once housed the previous owner's pack of hounds. The dogs followed into the pen and flopped down on the straw with a variety of doggy sighs.

"Would you, Miss Cassie? Not that I think he'd beat me or anything."

"Of course he wouldn't." He wasn't Rodney Gilbert, after all. "But yes. I'll wait in his office and tell about the dogs. Will you feed and water them?"

"Course I will. I can see they've had a run." Jemmy ran off to get what was needed, and Cassie led Brummell back out into the stable yard and watched him lope back into the darkened parkland.

The steward's office was dark and empty. And decidedly chilly. A fire had been laid, so Cassie picked up the tinderbox and struck a spark. As soon as the kindling ignited, she lit two of the lamps and settled down to wait for Geoffrey.

Chapter 12

It had been a long, hard day. Geoffrey had spent it in the saddle under the strong May sun, riding through the fields with Tom Crocker. Geoffrey had brought back several suggestions from a trip to Norfolk the previous winter, and the farmer had been interested in Geoffrey's suggestions on what to plant. Crocker had agreed on most, but some changes had required an argument, a fact that bespoke Crocker's love of the land and of his job. Geoffrey felt that the home farm was in good hands.

The sun had already set when Geoffrey slid from his saddle to the cobbled yard and stood for a moment, absently patting his horse and gazing at the dusky silhouette of Bradworth Hall. Geoffrey had never realized how beautiful the house was. A stable boy ran out to take his horse and Geoffrey gratefully handed him over. Lord, but he was tired. But there was work to be done before he could seek his bed. Brushing some of the dust from his buckskins, Geoffrey headed toward his office.

Light glinted through the rippled glass of the estate office windows. As Geoffrey lifted the latch, he made a mental note to thank Mrs. Woodruff for lighting the lamp and starting the fire. It was a chilly night.

The lamplight pooled on his desk, illuminating the ledger he had left open that morning and a small stack of correspondence that must have been delivered while he was out in the fields. The corners of the room were already in shadow, but Geoffrey moved straight toward the small cot he kept in the room for late evenings. He longed to drop down on it and sleep but, for the moment, would settle for kicking off his boots.

As he approached the dark corner, a slight movement caught his eye. Geoffrey stepped back and picked up the lamp on his desk. He swung around toward the cot and nearly dropped the light. Cassie Hartwell, hair tousled and face creased, had risen to her knees on the bed, a confused expression on her lovely face.

Cassie rubbed her eyes and took a deep breath.

Before she could say anything, Geoffrey raised his free hand. "Do not speak."

Cassie's eyes widened, but she obeyed, dropping back to a sitting position and folding her hands in her lap. She stared up at Geoffrey with a look of puzzled astonishment.

Geoffrey continued toward the cot and set the lamp down on the small table beside it. He stood for a long moment looking down into Cassie Hartwell's meadow-green eyes. He didn't know what had brought her to his room, and he was not sure he really cared.

Finding Cassie on his bed was a revelation. She was the last person he had expected to see there and the first person he would have wished to find. He was, at once, puzzled and jubilant. He had come home and she was here, waiting for him. It was exactly as it should be.

When he had realized it was Cassie on his bed, Geoffrey's heart told him that that was where he wanted her for the rest of his life. The very fact that Cassie was in his room warmed it and brought it alive, brought him alive.

It made no difference whose daughter she was. Then and there, Geoffrey knew that one day she would be the Duchess of Passmore. And who would say her nay? He was done fighting his attraction to the vicar's daughter. She was *the one*.

Geoffrey regarded the solemn little face peering up at him and relished the blush creeping over the already-rosy cheeks. When Cassie looked as though she might say something, Geoffrey dropped to the cot beside her and, taking her shoulders in his hands, turned her to face him.

When she opened her lips to speak, Geoffrey sealed them with his. This was the kiss. Anything that had gone before—the brief, stolen kiss on the terrace of Gilbert Grange, the sweet interlude at the fair—was just practice. This was the kiss that a man gives the woman he loves.

He molded his lips to Cassie's and she responded as if she were the other half of him. Their lips met and clung. Their breath mingled and became one. Their hearts found each other's cadence and made it a single beat.

Geoffrey slid his hands down Cassie's arms and gathered her to him without taking his mouth from hers. As he enfolded her, his lips gentled and coaxed, told her the tale of what was in his heart, bound her to him with promises of what could be. Within moments, Cassie softened against him, settling her arms around his neck and answering each of his kisses with one of her own.

Geoffrey groaned and leaned back against the wall. Cassie crawled into his lap, took his face between her capable hands, and kissed him with a fervor that took his breath away. Breaking away for a moment, he lowered her to the bed and then resumed his kiss, this time accompanying it with long, tender caresses that swept over her perfectly rounded body and set his own ablaze.

Her clothing was in the way, but it was not yet time to remove it. That time would come and, Geoffrey hoped, soon. For now, he contented himself with smoothing the fabric over her wonderful form and imagining the moment when he would finally free her soft skin to his touch.

Cassie's gentle murmurs turned to soft moans and Geoffrey knew that he had to pull back before they were both beyond stopping. He stilled his hands and, raising his head, gazed down at her.

"Geoffrey." Cassie murmured his name and Geoffrey lost himself in her passion-glazed eyes. Her voice was a husky whisper filled with wonder. She reached up and brushed back the hair that had fallen over his forehead.

"I . . ." Geoffrey couldn't finish the sentence. Before he could tell Cassie that he loved her, he had to tell her the truth. A confession of love should not be born from a web of lies. First he would explain, and then he would marry her.

Instead, Geoffrey bent his head and kissed each of her eyelids and then the tip of her nose. "Why are you here?"

"Oh my!" Pushing at his chest, Cassie wrenched herself upright. She sprang from the bed and whirled back toward him. Geoffrey pulled himself off the cot to face her.

"Oh my," she said again, biting her lips and twisting her hands at her waist. "I have . . . I have done something . . . well . . . not wrong." She stopped, her expression wavering between pugnacious and pleading. "I have done something not quite legal."

Geoffrey smiled. "How not quite legal?"

"Do not laugh at me." Cassie folded her arms across her chest, immediately drawing Geoffrey's attention to the generous curves he had stroked only minutes before. He could think of several things he would rather do than laugh.

Cassie flounced past him and leaned against the corner of his desk. "I have stolen Mr. Rodney Gilbert's dogs."

"What?" Geoffrey sank back onto the bed.

"I have stolen Mr. Gilbert's dogs." Cassie stuck her chin out at a stubborn angle.

Overcome with a sudden desire to kiss the dimple her expression created, Geoffrey left the cot and strode to where Cassie stood. Grasping her narrow waist, he lifted her from the floor and sat her on his desk. Then, he placed his lips against her cheek and investigated the inviting concavity near her mouth.

"Did you hear me?" Cassie pushed at his shoulder.

"I did." Geoffrey kissed the dimple on the other side.

"I brought them here."

Geoffrey stopped kissing her and backed up a bit to examine her face. "You are serious."

"Quite." Cassie slid off the desk and paced to the door and back.

When Cassie stood before Geoffrey again, he took both her hands in his and pulled her toward him until their bodies were almost touching. "This is not good," he said, quietly.

Cassie dropped her gaze to the floor. "I know."

Geoffrey waited until she raised her head again. He said nothing, knowing that she would tell him everything without being asked.

"He was beating them," she said, finally, her eyes brimming.

Geoffrey raised a hand and gently brushed a tear from her lash. His dear, gentle, loving Cassie. Of course she would not tolerate anyone abusing animals.

"Could you not have reported this to the magistrate?" It was the most logical course.

Cassie gulped back her tears. "Sir Edmund?"

The name spoke volumes. Gilbert's uncle and, to Geoffrey's mind, not the most sympathetic of men.

"I see," he said. "Where are they?" Geoffrey kept his tone soft. It was important that Cassie understand he was not angry.

"Jemmy Crocker put them in an empty box stall. The one the old lord used as his kennel."

Geoffrey blew out a considering breath and, taking Cassie's hand, walked her to the old leather chair behind the desk and sat her down. Then, he did some pacing of his own. After several circuits of the room, he stopped midstride and turned to face his dog thief.

"How did you get them here?"

Cassie raised her shoulders and gave him a sheepish smile.

Geoffrey laughed. "You just opened the pen and they followed you." Even without closing his eyes, Geoffrey could conjure up a vivid image of Cassie Hartwell tramping across the fields followed by an adoring pack of hounds. Well, who could blame them?

"Oh, Cassie." Geoffrey walked around the desk and knelt beside her, stroking her arm.

"I'm sorry," she whispered. "I didn't know where else to take them."

Geoffrey leaned forward and put his arms around her. "Hush. Of course you should have brought them to me. You must bring all of your troubles to me."

Cassie exhaled deeply and collapsed against Geoffrey. She had been so afraid that he would be angry and now she was afraid that she had brought him serious trouble.

And she loved him. She had thought for a while that she did, but she had known for sure the moment he had kissed her. Or maybe the moment before, when she sat up on his cot and realized where she was and who was with her. She loved him and she had made him her accomplice. No good could come from this.

Cassie didn't realize she was crying until she felt Geoffrey push his handkerchief into her hand. He was making soft, hushing noises and cradling her against his broad chest. She felt safe and protected. She felt as if no harm could come to her as long as Geoffrey had his arms around her. She blew her nose and sat up straighter. It was not like her to succumb to tears.

She sensed Geoffrey's reluctance to let her go, but she needed to stand on her own for a minute. She needed to feel her own strength before she could go on. Loving Geoffrey would be a disaster if it meant giving up her own nature. Gently, she pulled away from him and rose from the chair.

"I have likely caused problems by bringing the

dogs here. I know that. But you know I had nowhere else to bring them." Cassie moved to the other side of the desk so she could continue speaking without touching Geoffrey.

"I do know that." Geoffrey nodded.

"I will make this right," Cassie said with more resolution than she felt at the moment. "But right now, I must leave before I compromise you even further."

She saw Geoffrey look around and knew the moment he realized their predicament. It was full dark, and Cassie had been alone with him for nearly an hour. She had to leave now.

"I will see you home." The quiet words raised a clamor in Cassie's chest.

"No!" She held up her hand to emphasize the imperative. "I must return home alone. I will not have it otherwise."

"Why? You must know . . ." Geoffrey's words trailed off.

Cassie fetched the shawl that had been pushed to the foot of the cot. "What I know or think I know must wait until we are both calmer. I do not want to create any false expectations or extract any promises right now. Do you understand?"

Geoffrey shook his head. "Not precisely."

"Men!" Cassie rolled her eyes and hurried toward the door.

"Wait." In two long strides, Geoffrey was in front of her, his hand against the door. "What do you mean?"

Cassie raised one hand and ran it along Geoffrey's cheek, savoring the harsh feel of a man many hours past his morning shave. "I mean that there are some things women see more clearly. I mean we need to wait and talk another day when we are not

trying to manage a pack of hounds. I mean I do not
want to try to explain to my mother why you are
seeing me home."

Geoffrey let his hand fall to his side. "I propose
a bargain, then. I will take you as far as the High
Street and watch until you are in your house. And
then what you tell your mother will be your affair."

Cassie opened her mouth to protest, but Geoffrey cut her off with a kiss. It was so sudden and so
sweet that it stole every thought from her head. She
grasped the front of his jacket and, standing on tiptoe, leaned into him, extracting every bit of tenderness from his pliant lips.

She could feel a moment of protest run through
her body. She was trying to make a point and he
was distracting her. So be it. No dissent, no point,
no opposition was nearly as engrossing as the firm
warmth of Geoffrey's mouth. Let him distract her.
Let him do whatever he desired with her. Cassie
murmured her acquiescence.

When the kiss ended, Geoffrey said, "I will not,
under any circumstances, allow you to make your
way home by yourself. Not now. Not in the dark."

Cassie nodded and stepped back. Geoffrey opened
the door and strode toward the stable block.

Cassie expected Geoffrey to return with a gig and
was surprised when he trotted up on a single horse.

Geoffrey directed the horse to the mounting
block and leaned down to her. "Climb up here, put
your foot on my boot, and give me your hand."

Beyond arguing, Cassie did as she was bid and
found herself cradled between Geoffrey Dorton's
muscular thighs. Leaning against the broad ex-
panse of his chest, she breathed a heartfelt sigh.

"Is that resignation?" Geoffrey asked with a smile
in his voice.

"That's contentment." Cassie snuggled close and prepared to enjoy the ride home.

Cassie savored every moment until Geoffrey let her down from his horse within sight of the vicarage. For she knew that whatever happened when she walked into the house after dark would not be in the least enjoyable.

How right she was. Mrs. Hartwell stood in the entryway, her hands on her hips and her face a mask of disapproval. Cassie glanced quickly toward her father's study. The sliver of lamplight under the door told her he was deep into his books and would be no help.

"Where have you been, young lady?" Mrs. Hartwell did not move, blocking any escape from the narrow hallway.

Cassie locked her gaze on her mother's face and said nothing. She should have spent the ride concocting an excuse rather than snuggling up to Geoffrey Dorton's irresistible chest.

"Well?" Mrs. Hartwell's right foot tapped twice on the worn planks of the floor.

"I . . . I stopped to see Miss Babson on the way home and lost track of the time." Cassie hoped that Miss Babson had not broken with her usual habit of locking herself into her cottage as soon as darkness fell.

Mrs. Hartwell raised an eyebrow. "That was quite a long visit."

"Well, I spent rather more time with Mrs. Smith than usual. She felt like reminiscing tonight." That, at least, was not a lie.

"Where is your basket?" Mrs. Hartwell's gaze

flickered to Cassie's hands and then returned to an examination of her face.

Oh Lord! Where was her basket? The last time she remembered having it was when she fed the cheese to the hounds at Gilbert Grange. "I must have left it at Mrs. Smith's."

"I'll send one of the boys to fetch it tomorrow." Mrs. Hartwell stepped back to allow Cassie to pass.

"No, I'll go get it. I think she would enjoy another visit." Cassie's heart beat a wild tattoo. She hoped she had left it at Mrs. Smith's, but she could not be sure it wasn't in Geoffrey's office or, worse, in the Gilbert Grange kennels. She stepped around her mother and was headed for the stairs when Mrs. Hartwell's hand shot out and grasped her upper arm.

"I have always trusted you, Cassie. I hope you will not make me rue that confidence."

Cassie gave her mother a quick hug and then ran up the stairs, entirely sure that nothing she had done in the past three hours would make her mother happy. She hated that.

Chapter 13

Geoffrey rolled over and embraced his pillow. If he inhaled deeply, he could still smell the scent of apple blossoms that clung to Cassie Hartwell's ebullient curls. He had slept on his narrow office cot, reluctant to abandon the spot where he had held Cassie in his arms for such a short, sweet time.

The problem with sleeping in the steward's office, however, was the lack of a morning fire. Even during planting season, the days in Devon started off with a chill. And, if his ears did not deceive him, it was raining. Geoffrey pulled the thin coverlet up to his chin and contemplated what his morning would have been like were he back in London at Passmore House or in the country on his father's estate.

A footman would have crept into his room and lit the fire before he awoke. At the requested hour, the curtains would have been drawn back to admit the morning sun and he would have been offered a cup of steaming coffee. He would have been cushioned in a feather-bed and covered by a down-filled quilt.

The only thing missing from this vision of comfort was the presence of Miss Cassie Hartwell. Geoffrey's body warmed as her image floated across his mind's eye. He knew with absolute certainty that he would rather spend his life waking up on a hard bed in a steward's cottage with Cassie than waking in the midst of luxury without her.

Indeed, the greatest luxury he could imagine was Cassie's companionship for the rest of his life. Geoffrey was determined to win that luxury, but he must start with a clean slate, must tell Cassie who he was and how much he loved her.

Rolling onto his back, Geoffrey slid his hands behind his head and stared at the rough ceiling. He must tell Cassie that one day he would be the Duke of Passmore. His heart misgave him as he considered how she would respond to this news.

He had lied to her, to all of Oakleigh, about who he was, and this would not sit well with the straightforward Miss Hartwell. He did not doubt that her mother would be in alt to have her daughter a duchess. But Cassie was such an independent little thing that he suspected it might not be quite so easy to convince her they should marry. Geoffrey shrugged his doubts aside. It was unthinkable that he would not succeed in winning her.

As Geoffrey sat up and swung his legs over the side of the cot, the courtyard outside his office erupted in a cacophony of voices. Men, dogs, horses joined in a chorus of confusion. It took little more than a second for Geoffrey to come fully awake and recognize the cause of the noise. Rodney Gilbert had come for his hounds.

Geoffrey pulled on his breeches and was reaching for his shirt when the noise subsided, followed by a sharp rap on the door.

"Mr. Dorton, are you in there?" Well, then. Not only Rodney Gilbert but his uncle as well.

"In a moment." Geoffrey tugged his shirt over his head and, tucking it in, started for the door. As he reached for the latch, Geoffrey happened to glance down. Cassie Hartwell's basket sat beside the door, testimony to her visit last night.

"Just coming," Geoffrey called to forestall another knock and quickly carried the basket back to the bed. He shoved it beneath the cot and pulled the coverlet forward until it draped over the edge of the bed to the floor. Satisfied that there was nothing else of Cassie's to be found in the room, Geoffrey threw the latch and pulled open the door.

"Sir Edmund." Geoffrey ran his hand through his hair, wishing he'd had time to shave and don some clean clothes. It was so much easier to face trouble when one was properly attired.

Sir Edmund hovered on the threshold, clearing his throat and looking indecisive. Behind him, his nephew glared at Geoffrey, his customary sneer almost quivering with joy. Geoffrey could tell that nothing could have made Rodney Gilbert happier than finding his dogs in Geoffrey's possession.

Taking a last, quick glance around the room, Geoffrey pulled the door fully opened and gestured toward the interior. "Won't you come in?"

Sir Edmund took a tentative step forward and then stumbled into the room as Gilbert shouldered past him.

Rodney Gilbert strode several feet into Geoffrey's office, then turned and folded his arms in an attitude of aggrieved belligerence.

"Please forgive the state of my office and . . . myself." Geoffrey looked down at his bare feet and grimaced.

"Yes . . . er . . . well . . ."

"Get on with it, Uncle." Without taking his eyes off Geoffrey, Gilbert returned to Sir Edmund's side.

"Er . . . Mr. Dorton. We have discovered my

nephew's dogs in your . . . that is to say, in the Bradworth stables."

Geoffrey raised an eyebrow, but did not answer. What, indeed, was there to say to that? Of course they had found the dogs here.

"Do you deny that they were here?" Rodney Gilbert puffed out his narrow chest.

"Now, Rodney, you must allow me to do this in my own way." Sir Edmund attempted to pat his nephew.

Rodney yanked his arm away but settled into disgruntled silence.

Sir Edmund returned to Geoffrey. "It's a good question, though. Eh, Mr. Dorton? Did you know my nephew's dogs were at Bradworth?"

Ignoring the sullen Mr. Gilbert, Geoffrey addressed the older man with exquisite courtesy. "I did."

"So you admit you took them?" Unable to keep his countenance, Rodney Gilbert burst into the conversation.

Geoffrey waited for Sir Edmund to rephrase the question.

"Did you take the dogs, Mr. Dorton?"

Geoffrey hesitated. It was critical he answer this question properly. He could not confess to stealing the dogs, nor would he say anything that might cast suspicion on Cassie. Indeed, it seemed best that they suspect him.

"I did not say that," he said after a significant pause.

"Ha!" Rodney Gilbert nudged his uncle with his elbow. "He's lying."

Sir Edmund had the grace to look abashed at Rodney's behavior, but that did not prevent him from continuing his questions.

"What, precisely, did you say?"

"I said I knew the dogs were here." Geoffrey gazed steadily at Sir Edmund, well aware that continued recalcitrance would likely cause the old man an apoplexy.

Sir Edmund inhaled deeply and relaxed the death grip he had taken on his walking stick. His color was still verging on puce. "Do you know how they got here?"

"I was not at home when they arrived."

"When they arrived? You make it sound as if they dropped by for tea." Sir Edmund's color deepened a shade.

"They might have done." Geoffrey turned to Rodney Gilbert. "You must have left your pen open."

"There, nephew." At last Sir Edmund's color began to subside. "A perfectly reasonable explanation. No harm done."

"I did *not* leave the pen open. I *never* leave the pen open. And this man is in possession of my hounds. I insist he be brought in for theft."

"Well . . . er . . . someone must have been here when the dogs—er—arrived. Put your boots on, Mr. Dorton, and meet us at the stables."

"No!" For the first time since the Gilberts had arrived, Geoffrey knew fear. "I'll just accompany you as I am."

Sir Edmund threw a quizzical look at Geoffrey's bare feet and shrugged. "As you will."

The rain had stopped for a moment, but the cobblestones were wet and slippery. Although the wet stones were cold against his soles, Geoffrey thought he might have better purchase in his bare feet than his visitors had in their leather boots. Geoffrey suppressed a snort as Rodney Gilbert suddenly slid on the stones, his arms windmilling as he regained his balance.

George Kingsley came out to greet the men. He had been in charge of the Bradworth stables for many years under the former owner, and Geoffrey had been glad when he agreed to stay on.

"Mr. Dorton, Sir Edmund . . . Mr. Gilbert."

Geoffrey was instantly aware that his stableman held Rodney Gilbert in particularly low regard.

"George, these gentlemen have come to get their dogs." The best thing that could happen would be for Rodney Gilbert to reclaim his hounds and leave Bradworth.

"I want more than my dogs," Rodney said in a nasal whine.

"Er, yes, Kingsley. We'd like to speak to whoever was here when the dogs . . . um . . . arrived." Sir Edmund peered around the man into the stable.

"That would be Jemmy Crocker, I think. Let me see if he's still here." Kingsley looked up at the sky. "You'd better come in," he added before disappearing through the door.

The three men stepped into the stable. They were instantly enveloped by the darkened interior and surrounded by the soft sound of whickering horses and the ineffable scent of clean horseflesh. Geoffrey sniffed appreciatively. Kingsley kept an immaculate stable.

A short bark sounded at the far end of the stable. Rodney Gilbert's head whipped around and he started in the direction of the sound. His uncle put his hand out to stop him. "Let us wait until we talk to the boy."

"I suppose a few minutes makes no difference." Rodney shrugged and fell back.

Soon, George Kingsley appeared, trailed by

young Jemmy Crocker. Kingsley put his hand on the boy's shoulder as they approached the three men waiting by the door.

"Here's Jemmy," Kingsley said, leaving his hand where it rested.

Geoffrey's heart fell. He had hoped the boy was gone and that there would be time to talk before he said anything that might implicate Cassie.

Jemmy pulled at his forelock and waited in silence.

"Were you here last night, boy?" Sir Edmund stepped forward, as did Rodney. Geoffrey hung back and tried to communicate with the lad without speaking.

"Yes, sir," Jemmy said, staring first at his feet and then over Sir Edmund's shoulder at Geoffrey.

"Did you see who brought the dogs?"

Geoffrey gave his head a slight shake, hoping that it was enough to tell Jemmy what he wanted him to do without alerting the Gilberts that he was prompting the boy.

"The dogs, sir?" Jemmy looked confused.

"Mr. Gilbert's hounds. The ones we can hear baying down there." Sir Edmund gestured toward the west end of the stable.

"Oh." Jemmy glanced quickly at Geoffrey and then straightened his shoulders. "No, sir. Didn't see nothin' but the dogs."

Geoffrey closed his eyes in a silent prayer of thanks. When this was all over, Jemmy was due a reward.

Sir Edmund was clearly skeptical. "The dogs just waltzed up to you by themselves?"

"No waltzing, sir. I opened the door and they were in the yard." The boy drew himself up proudly. "I gave them a right nice place to sleep."

"Uncle." Rodney Gilbert's patience was wearing thin.

"We cannot prove anything, Rodney." Sir Edmund nodded to the stable boy. Thank you . . . er . . . young man."

Jemmy looked up at the stable master and, at his nod, ran off across the shiny cobbles.

Sir Edmund turned to leave, but was stopped by his nephew. "I want justice. You must make an arrest."

"Rodney." Sir Edmund ran his hand through the few strands of hair atop his head.

"I insist."

The squire sighed. "Very well. Mr. Dorton, if you will be so kind as to . . . um . . . finish dressing, you will have to come with me. Rodney, fetch your dogs."

"Of course." Relieved that Cassie had not been mentioned, Geoffrey was happy to do anything he was asked.

Chapter 14

Cassie slowly swam to consciousness. The patter of rain against her window pulled her out of a glorious dream: a dream of strong arms and tender kisses, a dream unlike any she had ever had, and unlike any she had ever hoped to have.

Squinting toward the window, Cassie tried to determine what time it was. The sky was too gray to tell. She flopped back onto her pillow, still drugged by her blissful dream. Gradually, reality filtered into the room.

She had known that Rodney Gilbert wasn't kind, but she had not been certain that he beat his dogs until she saw it yesterday as she crossed one of the Gilbert Grange fields. Last night's events came back to her in a wave of emotion.

When Cassie had finally gained her bed, sleep had not come easily. Her mind roiled with myriad emotions. She lay immobile, counting the cracks in her ceiling as she revisited every one of the steps that had brought her to Bradworth Hall that night. And with each step, she wondered what she might have done differently. What would have saved the dogs and not involved Geoffrey? What might she have done that would not have made it necessary to lie to her mother?

She finally slept only to wake with the same refrain running through her mind and the same certainty that she had done only what she must.

Every time she thought about absconding with Rodney Gilbert's dogs, her heart pounded and her face burned. It had been impossible for her to leave them to undergo further abuse, but she could not imagine a path out of the coil into which she had got Geoffrey and herself.

Eventually, Cassie's mind had calmed, her panic over the dogs overtaken by the memory of lying in Geoffrey's arms. She fancied she could still smell him on her skin, still feel his lips, like silk against hers. She snuggled deeper into her mattress, clinging to the echo of Geoffrey's embrace.

Cassie stretched and pulled herself upright. What time was it? The sound of Dora's footsteps in the hallway indicated that the household was awake. She swung her legs over the side of the bed. Over the steady beat of the rain, she could just hear the murmur of voices from downstairs.

Cassie washed and dressed herself in a serviceable lavender day dress that she vaguely remembered being white when her sister Eleanor wore it. Her parents were already at the table as Cassie slid into her accustomed chair.

"I always said there was something about him I could not like." Mrs. Hartwell leaned toward her husband as she spoke.

"I, for one, do not believe a word of it." Reverend Hartwell's brow was drawn up in a puzzled frown.

"Too handsome for his own good. Thinks he can do anything that comes into his head." Mrs. Hartwell picked up her toast and applied butter as if it were a punishment.

Cassie's heart dropped. "Who are you talking about?"

"Your Mr. Dorton," her mother said, accusation dripping from every word.

Cassie froze in the midst of reaching for the toast. *Her Mr. Dorton.* She was quite sure her mother didn't mean that in the way Cassie now thought it.

"What has happened?" Cassie knew her voice would give her away, but there was no way to disguise her distress.

"Stole Mr. Gilbert's—" Mrs. Hartwell had not finished her sentence before her husband interrupted.

"Mr. Dorton has been accused of stealing Mr. Gilbert's dogs. That does not mean"—he glanced at his wife—"that he has stolen them."

"He hasn't." Cassie's words emerged in a breathless squeak.

"Of course he has," Mrs. Hartwell said.

"How can you know that?" Mr. Hartwell asked at the same time.

Cassie looked down at her lap, where she had twisted her napkin into a tight knot. "I stole the dogs."

"Nonsense." Mrs. Hartwell rose from the table and stalked to where Cassie sat.

"It's true, Mama." Cassie craned her neck to look up at her mother, who was now looming over her. "I saw Mr. Gilbert beating them and I couldn't bear it. I took them and I put them in the Bradworth kennels."

"Sit down, Amelia."

Mr. Hartwell rarely used his wife's given name,

and it was sure to get her attention. Cassie cast a grateful glance at her father.

Mrs. Hartwell returned to her seat but continued to glare at her daughter. "I will not have you perjure yourself for this . . . person, no matter how handsome you think him."

"I will not perjure myself." Cassie put her crumpled napkin on her plate and pushed herself away from the table. "Where is Mr. Dorton?"

"Dora says they've taken him to Gilbert Grange. Sir Edmund is the magistrate, you know." Mrs. Hartwell's face expressed satisfaction at this state of affairs.

If possible, Cassie's heart sank even lower. Of course, Sir Edmund was the magistrate. How could she have forgotten? How could she have even imagined that this precipitous action would not come before the law?

"I must go to Gilbert Grange."

"You are going nowhere, miss." Mrs. Hartwell was on her feet again, her hands on her hips.

Cassie turned to her father. "Surely you see I must go. I cannot let them accuse Ge—Mr. Dorton of something he did not do."

"You must wait until the rain lets up." Mr. Hartwell also rose from his seat and came around the table to put an arm about Cassie's shoulders.

"Mr. Hartwell!"

"Cassie must go and say her piece, but I will not have her contract a lung fever while she is doing it." Cassie had never heard her father sound so firm outside of the pulpit. Her heart swelled in gratitude. Her father had come to her aid when she most needed a champion.

Cassie watched her mother huff and sweep out of

the room, then turned back to her father, who was regarding her with worry in his eyes.

"Is what you say the truth, daughter, or are you protecting Mr. Dorton?"

"It's true, Papa. I never meant this to happen, but you know I could not let Mr. Gilbert beat those dogs." Cassie's eyes filled with tears.

Mr. Hartwell hugged her. "I know, my dear. I know. But I beg you to be circumspect when you speak with Sir Edmund. He can be . . . er . . . opinionated."

"Yes, Papa." Cassie allowed herself to be enfolded in her father's gentle embrace, but her mind raced. She had to get to Gilbert Grange and she was not entirely sure she could bear to wait for the rain to stop.

Geoffrey paced the floor of the small back chamber into which he had been locked. He should not have been surprised when Sir Edmund and Rodney Gilbert came for him this morning. And yet he was.

It was all Cassie Hartwell's fault. Not her fault that he was arrested—although he supposed that should be laid at her feet as well. If his mind had not been so full of her startling green eyes, her delightful halo of chestnut curls, her beguiling little body, and her infectious smile, he would have remembered that he was harboring stolen dogs.

Geoffrey stopped at the window and looked down into the garden. It was not a long drop and the window was easily unlatched. The Gilberts obviously did not have much experience as jailers.

He gave the windowpane a little tap and returned to his pacing. He should be worrying about more important things than the security of his makeshift prison. He needed to determine how to get himself out of this mess without implicating

Cassie. At the moment, he couldn't think of a single solution.

The torrential rain subsided into a soft drizzle and still Geoffrey had no answer. He had been left alone for over an hour to consider his sins, so he supposed the Gilberts had no clear idea of what to do with him.

Geoffrey was beginning to wonder if he had been left alone in the house, when he heard the clatter of wheels on the slate in the front courtyard and the sound of doors opening and closing.

Cassie abandoned her cart and pony and, without a backward glance, strode up the shallow sandstone steps to Gilbert Grange. She shivered as she waited for someone to answer the knock. The rain had started up again right after she left the vicarage, but she refused to turn back, and now she was damp through to her chemise.

When Sir Edmund himself opened the door, she realized she was too out of breath to speak.

"Miss Cassie. Come in. Come in." Sir Edmund flung the door wide and took Cassie's hand. "Whatever is the matter?"

"Oh, Sir Edmund." Cassie stopped to gulp in some air. "I have come about Mr. Dorton."

"Tush, child. That's none of your concern." Sir Edmund closed the door and reached for Cassie's shawl.

Cassie clutched the damp fabric tightly around her and shook her head. "But it is," she said. "I took the dogs."

"You took the dogs? What nonsense." Rodney Gilbert's nasal voice issued from the entrance to the west wing. Cassie swung around to face him as he sauntered into the entry hall.

"It is quite true." Cassie heard the quaver in her voice and clenched her fists, marshalling her resolve. She raised her chin and looked directly into Rodney Gilbert's narrowed eyes.

"I could not bear to let you beat them."

Cassie expected Mr. Gilbert to deny the accusation. Instead, he shrugged. "They're my property. It's no one's business what I do with them."

"So you admit that I saw you beat the dogs?"

Gilbert shrugged again. "Might have."

"Then you must acknowledge that I am the one who took them." Cassie grimaced to keep her teeth from chattering, unsure whether the cause was her damp shawl or the anxiety pervading every nerve in her body.

"I said 'nonsense' and nonsense it is. No woman could have moved those hounds. Takes a man with a strong arm to manage them."

Cassie felt the blood rush to her face. Rodney Gilbert would never believe a woman could do something he could not manage himself. She would get nowhere with the thick-skulled coxcomb. She turned to his uncle. "You must believe me. Mr. Dorton has done nothing wrong."

Sir Edmund patted her on the shoulder, quickly removing his dampened hand and wiping it on his jacket. "You are too kindhearted, Miss Cassie. I know you mean well, but we found the dogs at Bradworth Hall, and Mr. Dorton has not denied he took them."

"Let me speak with him." Cassie ground her teeth in frustration.

"I can't do that, Miss Hartwell." The squire was suddenly his most officious. "It will not do to allow a gently bred young lady such as yourself to speak with a criminal."

Cassie almost stamped her foot. "I tell you he is no criminal. I am."

"Go home to your mother, my dear, and have Dora make you up one of her tisanes. Won't do to have the vapors."

"The vapors?" Cassie's voice rose in outrage. She had no control over the situation, but she could not just turn tail and leave Geoffrey—where? Cassie stepped back from Sir Edmund. Where was Geoffrey? Perhaps there was another means of helping him.

Sir Edmund's already wrinkled forehead creased further as he studied Cassie's sudden silence.

Cassie cleared her throat. "Tell me, Sir Edmund. Where are you holding the . . . ah . . . miscreant?"

Sir Edmund's puzzled frown eased. "None of that," he said, shaking his head. "I'll not have you sneaking around after the prisoner."

At the word *prisoner*, Cassie's anger returned in full force. She rounded again on Rodney Gilbert. "Do not think that you will get away with hurting animals here in Oakleigh. And do not think that I will allow you to call on me again."

Mr. Gilbert looked over Cassie's shoulder at his uncle. Cassie glanced back in time to see Sir Edmund shaking his head in warning.

"Never fear, Miss Hartwell. I have no desire to call upon a young lady who is sniffing after the likes of a lawless land steward." Mr. Gilbert had obviously decided to ignore his uncle. "In fact, my dear, do not flatter yourself that I could not do much better than you. I acted only to please Sir Edmund."

For some reason, this information not only relieved Cassie's mind, it made a great deal of sense.

She and Rodney Gilbert had never liked each other. His persistent courtship had been both puzzling and annoying. Only her mother's persistent worry about Cassie's prospects had convinced her to put up with his company.

"You are speaking nonsense, Rodney. And impolite nonsense at that." Sir Edmund glared at his nephew before turning a conciliatory smile on Cassie. "I hope you two will make this up. Your mama and I have such high hopes for a match."

A match? How had this discussion strayed so far from her purpose? Cassie's only candidate for a match was, at this moment, languishing somewhere in Gilbert Grange, locked up in consequence of Cassie's own foolishness. She would accomplish nothing here, but she was not done with this. She returned to her mission with vigor.

Chapter 15

The door to Geoffrey's room cracked open, and Geoffrey recognized Sir Edmund's beady eye surveying the makeshift prison.

"I promise not to attack you," he called, seating himself in a chair as far away from the door as possible and extending his legs in a pose of nonchalance.

Sir Edmund slipped into the room and closed the door behind him.

Geoffrey maintained his pose, leaning back in the chair and eyeing the older gentleman, waiting for him to speak.

Sir Edmund shuffled to the window and examined the fastenings, much as Geoffrey had done earlier in the day. He must have reached a different conclusion about their security, for he turned back to Geoffrey with a satisfied smile.

"You know I must keep you here until . . ." Sir Edmund stopped, a perplexed frown forming on his face.

"Until?"

"Ah yes. Well, I'm very sorry for it, but there must be a summary hearing." Sir Edmund's brow wrinkled in apology.

"Must there, indeed?" Geoffrey could not help feeling some sympathy for the squire. He obviously would rather not be holding anyone prisoner in his home.

"Well . . . yes. I'm afraid Rodney insists. And he is the victim after all."

"Yes, I suppose he is," Geoffrey said, sitting upright in the chair and grasping the arms.

Sir Edmund flinched and stepped back a pace.

Geoffrey smiled. "I promised not to attack you. Remember?"

Sir Edmund gave a nervous laugh. "Silly of me. But we don't get much of this sort of thing in Oakleigh."

"What sort of thing is that? Runaway dogs?" Even as he spoke Geoffrey knew that, in some corner of the law, Rodney Gilbert was perfectly justified in seeking to punish someone for the theft of his hounds. And Geoffrey was determined that, if a party was punished, it would not be Cassie Hartwell.

As Sir Edmund's agitation seemed to be increasing at every moment, Geoffrey did not pursue the conversation. Instead, he picked up a piece of paper from the desk.

"I assumed you would want to keep me here. Would you be so kind as to have this delivered to Mrs. Woodruff?"

Sir Edmund took the folded paper from Geoffrey's hand and held it out before him.

"You may read it." Geoffrey took the sheet back and opened it before handing it back to the squire. "I have only asked for some clothes and made a list of the tasks that must be done at Bradworth within the next few days. I hope to be out of here by then."

"Oh, quite. Of course." Sir Edmund nodded. "I'll ju   ave this delivered. And of course, I'll have your supper sent up." He looked around the room. "You won't try to . . ."

Geoffrey dropped back into the chair. "I have been here all day and will remain here at your convenience," he said, adding as Sir Edmund opened the door to leave, "I would appreciate something to read, however. It is quite dull in here with only my own company."

Supper arrived along with a two-week-old London newspaper and a tome on hog farming written in 1743. It was going to be a very long night. Geoffrey put the newspaper on top, reasoning that, even two weeks past, it would be more current, and undoubtedly more interesting, than a seventy-year-old book on hogs.

The meal was not fancy, but Geoffrey imagined that the mutton in the Oxford John was of a relatively recent vintage and the pickled red cabbage was quite savory. All in all, it was a better meal than he would have been served in the Exeter jail.

Supper dispatched, Geoffrey flipped open the newspaper and scanned the columns. Gossip was rife regarding the regent's wife. There was rumor of providing her with an annuity as long as she remained out of England. The currency commission was recommending a return to gold payments. Parliament was still in session, and his father was busy, as usual. Even when the duke's name was not mentioned, Geoffrey recognized his fine hand steering some of the bills facing the House of Lords.

His sister Aurelia and her husband, Viscount Auburndale, were mentioned more than once and seemed to have become the toast of the season, seen at all the most glittering events.

Geoffrey continued scanning the pages, looking for Sarah, his older sister, and her husband, Lord

Marchbourn. They were nowhere to be found. He smiled as he turned the broadsheet to the next page. Sarah and Julian were likely already back in Somerset where they were happiest. Julian never liked to be too long away from his farms.

Snapping the paper shut, Geoffrey got to his feet and began to pace. How long would he be confined here? He had committed his time and effort to caring for Julian's newly acquired second estate, and the last thing he wanted to do was fail his brother-in-law. Julian had given Geoffrey a purpose and his life a direction at a time when he seemed headed for a sink of debauchery. He owed him more than he could ever repay.

It was certainly not Julian's fault that Geoffrey had chosen to enter Oakleigh under an assumed identity. Nor was it his fault that Geoffrey had made a cake of himself over the vicar's daughter and, in the process, alienated the squire's nephew.

Geoffrey returned to his chair and picked up the pig book. The newspaper was too vivid a reminder of the kind of life he had to look forward to. For the first time since finding Cassie Hartwell asleep on his cot, Geoffrey wondered what it would be like to take her to London.

Cassie was bright and funny and frighteningly independent. Geoffrey doubted that anything would cow her. But she was a country girl and seemed particularly happy right here in Devon. Would she be miserable if he picked her up and planted her in the arid soil of the *ton*, or would she thrive there as she had here?

For the first time since he'd come to the decision to marry Cassie, Geoffrey wondered if it would be the right thing to do for her. He leaned back in his chair and closed his eyes. Immediately, an image of

Cassie's luminous face and unruly curls formed in his mind.

As Geoffrey dwelt on the intelligent expression of her sparkling green eyes and the unbearable sweetness of her smile, he knew that he had no other choice. If he did not marry her, he would regret it for the rest of his life. His task was to ensure she did not regret it if he did.

His first task, however, was to get himself out of this mess without implicating Cassie. As yet, he had no clear idea of how that might be done. But he must find a solution before the summary hearing remanded him to trial. Once that process had started, weeks, possibly months, would be lost before it ended.

The only solution that presented itself was to negotiate a compromise with Rodney Gilbert. Surely Geoffrey was in a position to offer something Rodney might want. But first he must learn what that something might be.

Geoffrey had just decided that going to bed with the sun would be more interesting than reading about hog farming in the last century when he heard the key in the lock. Thinking that it must be the maid returning to collect his supper dishes, he went to the table to fetch them.

Thus, he was standing in the middle of the room with a stack of crockery in his hand when the door opened to admit Reverend Hartwell. Geoffrey immediately set the dishes back on the table and moved to greet the vicar. Looking over Mr. Hartwell's shoulder, he could see his host hovering in the hallway.

"Will you come in as well, Sir Edmund?" Geoffrey backed away from the door lest either gentleman think he was bent on escape.

Sir Edmund shook his head. "Not necessary, Dorton. Just come to let the vicar in to see you. Now behave yourself," he added as he pulled the door shut.

Geoffrey shook Mr. Hartwell's hand and offered him the chair, seating himself on the edge of the narrow bed once the vicar had made himself comfortable.

"I wish I had refreshment to offer you, sir."

Mr. Hartwell smiled and shook his head. "Not necessary and certainly not expected." He looked around the room. "This is not too terrible."

"All things considered, it certainly could have been worse." Geoffrey shrugged.

The two men sat in silence for several moments.

"Is there something I can do for you?" Geoffrey asked.

Mr. Hartwell rose and went to the window. Geoffrey watched his guest gaze out into the fading light. The rear window was certainly a surprising source of fascination.

Mr. Hartwell returned to the chair. "Cassie told me what happened."

Geoffrey raised an eyebrow.

The older man nodded. "You are not going to volunteer anything," he said with some satisfaction.

"No, sir."

"I think she's right about you." The vicar sat back in the chair and met Geoffrey's expectant gaze. "She told me she took Gilbert's dogs and brought them to Bradworth Hall."

Geoffrey still said nothing.

"My daughter told the truth."

It was not a question, but close enough to one to make the back of Geoffrey's neck prickle. "What would you have me say, Mr. Hartwell?"

The vicar studied Geoffrey's face for a moment.

"I believe I want you to do just as you have done, my boy."

Geoffrey shifted on the edge of the bed, trying to ease the tension in his shoulders. "Why are you here?"

"Something must be done. But I cannot risk my daughter's reputation. Surely you see that." Mr. Hartwell peered at Geoffrey from under his bushy brows. "Yes. Of course you do."

"Perhaps you could arrange a meeting for me with Mr. Gilbert. I think I might offer sufficient compensation for his . . . er . . . distress."

Mr. Hartwell's eyebrows shot to his hairline. "Can you, indeed?"

Geoffrey nodded. "Given enough time, I can muster considerable resources."

"Ah. Excellent, excellent." Mr. Hartwell paused and looked around the room once more. "Is there anything else I can do for you?"

Geoffrey shook his head. "I thank you. Just get me that interview."

"Well, then . . ." Mr. Hartwell stood and Geoffrey rose from the bed. The vicar held out his hand. "I will see what I can do with Mr. Gilbert."

Geoffrey shook the vicar's hand. "Thank you. And . . . when all this is behind us, I hope to speak to you on a happier matter."

Mr. Hartwell clapped Geoffrey on the shoulder. "I suspected you might."

Chapter 16

Rodney Gilbert appeared at his door as soon as the breakfast dishes had been cleared away. Mr. Hartwell was as good as his word, as Geoffrey had known he would be. Now it was up to Geoffrey to do his part.

He stood as Gilbert swaggered into the room. It would not do to antagonize the man when he wanted to win his agreement, and Geoffrey concluded that obsequiousness would serve him well with Rodney Gilbert.

Without being asked, Gilbert took the room's single chair and Geoffrey, as was fast becoming his custom, perched on the edge of the bed. Neither man spoke, and Geoffrey took the moment to observe his accuser. Rodney Gilbert was not ill-looking. In fact, Geoffrey was quite sure many considered him handsome. But he had a sly expression that had made Geoffrey distrust him from their first meeting, and further acquaintance had not changed his opinion.

Gilbert was nearly as tall as Geoffrey but of slighter build. He affected the dress and manner of a London dandy and, in Geoffrey's opinion, looked quite out of place as he lounged in his uncle's homely chair in the back bedroom of a modest country estate.

Geoffrey knew his type, had seen it often enough in town: a hanger-on of the fringes of the *ton*, aping the Corinthians, playing too deep and aspiring to heiresses and *demimondaines* he had no hope of winning. The very thought of the man with Cassie made Geoffrey's skin crawl.

Nevertheless, he schooled his expression to polite interest and asked Rodney Gilbert how he did.

"Glad to have my hounds back." Gilbert was obviously not in a mood to be conciliatory.

"Yes, well . . . that is what I wanted to speak to you about."

"Dare say you do. Do you no good, you know. I want justice." Gilbert's surly expression darkened into belligerence.

"I am prepared to offer you handsome compensation for the trouble you've been put through." Geoffrey bit down hard to prevent himself from telling the man what he thought of him.

"Handsome compensation? On steward's pay?" Gilbert looked amused by the very idea.

"I have . . . er . . . other resources."

"Do you, indeed? Perhaps this is something my uncle should look into. Might be some people missing their valuables." Gilbert's gaze sharpened with interest.

"I have my own funds." Geoffrey kept his voice low and calm, disgusted with the man and with this game. "Sir Edmund will find nothing of interest there."

Gilbert shrugged. "A man who would steal a pack of hounds . . ."

Geoffrey rose and strode toward Rodney Gilbert, coming to rest immediately before the chair on which he sat. He stood too close to allow the man to stand himself and close enough so that Gilbert was obliged to lean back and crane his neck in order to see Geoffrey's face.

"D-don't touch me."

"I have no intention of touching you, Mr. Gilbert." Geoffrey stood over him for another moment and then walked to the pitcher on the far side of the room and poured himself a cup of tepid water. "May I offer you some?" he asked, holding up the jug.

Shifting in the chair, Gilbert shook his head. "Why am I here, Dorton?"

Geoffrey returned to a position by the bed, but remained standing. "As I said, I wish to make restitution for your . . . inconvenience."

"Inconvenience you call it?" Gilbert shot to his feet.

"Very well, call it whatever you will. I wish to make it good."

"How much?"

"What do you think is equitable?" Geoffrey rocked slightly on the balls of his feet.

Gilbert glanced at Geoffrey's stance. "One thousand pounds."

"One thousand for a pack of hounds missing overnight?"

"One thousand pounds and your promise to have no more to do with Miss Hartwell."

"I beg your pardon?"

"You heard me." Rodney Gilbert smoothed an imaginary wrinkle from the arm of his jacket, and then turned his calculating gaze back on Geoffrey.

"What difference can this make to you?" Geoffrey could not suppress his desire to know.

The man raised his shoulders in a gesture of careless acknowledgment. "None, really. But it pleases my uncle to think I might marry her. And it pleases me to cater to my uncle. In any case, regardless of the reason, that is my price."

Lord, the man was petty. "Two thousand pounds and no promise." The sudden avidity in Gilbert's gaze made Geoffrey swear under his breath. He had given away more than he intended.

"Two thousand it is, but I still want the promise."

Grimacing, Geoffrey shook his head. This was an odd request and a very high price. He contemplated agreeing to the terms now, simply to rid himself of this problem. But there was no way he would commit to shunning Cassie. The two thousand pounds was no problem.

"I will need to return to Bradworth Hall." Once he had freedom of movement, Geoffrey would work out a solution that did not involve giving up the woman he loved.

"No." The response was immediate and flat. "You will stay here until the hearing unless you produce the agreed compensation." The statement was punctuated by the sound of the door slamming behind Rodney Gilbert, followed by the bolt falling into place.

Geoffrey sat on the bed with his head in his hands and rehearsed the conversation several times. How might he have handled it better? What would have convinced Rodney Gilbert to take the money and leave him to marry the one woman he wanted? How much money was enough? Was there an amount, or did Rodney Gilbert truly value his uncle's good opinion over ready cash? And how could Geoffrey discover these things while he was locked in a back chamber?

Rising, Geoffrey went to the window and tested the fastenings. They opened easily enough. He looked down the side of the house to the back garden. He could probably drop to the ground without breaking anything. Geoffrey pushed the window open. A cool breeze filtered into the room and ruffled the curtains. It carried the scent of grass after a spring rain and, in from a distance, the pungent aroma of fields recently plowed for planting.

Geoffrey pulled the window shut. Escaping out the back would mean giving up Bradworth and, possibly, Cassie. It would gain him nothing but the temporary feeling of the ground beneath his feet, a feeling sorely missed during his three days of confinement.

No. The only way to rectify the situation was to see it through. If he could not buy off Rodney Gilbert, and he had not entirely given up hope of doing that, then he would go to trial and pay the man after the fact. When he got to court, his identity was sure to come out and he could not imagine that the son of the Duke of Passmore would be jailed for borrowing some dogs.

Cassie rapped on the kitchen door at Bradworth Hall and listened as someone shuffled across the floor. The door creaked open and the housekeeper peered out, her wrinkled face brightening into a smile.

"Miss Cassie. Come in. Come in." Mrs. Woodruff swung the door wide and grasped Cassie's hand, pulling her into the warm kitchen. "I'm right glad to see you, miss. Have you seen Mr. Dorton? Is he well?"

The smell of freshly baked bread enveloped Cassie as the housekeeper led her toward the small table off to one side of the room. She inhaled deeply, relaxing into the comforting aroma. "I have not seen Mr. Dorton, but Father has, and says he is in good spirits."

The housekeeper nodded in satisfaction and set about slicing some of the warm bread. She arranged the slices on a platter and placed it on the table along with a crock of fresh butter. "Would you like some tea, dear?"

"No, I thank you, Mrs. Woodruff. I'm here because Papa says you have some things that must be delivered to Mr. Dorton. I'm to pick them up and take them to Gilbert Grange."

"Have some of my bread first. I've put a loaf in for Mr. Dorton, but I know how much you like it." Mrs. Woodruff pushed the platter toward Cassie.

Cassie slid a slice off the platter and slathered it with butter. She had never been able to resist Mrs. Woodruff's baking. "Just one slice."

"Have another, dear. I'll just go get Mr. Dorton's things." Mrs. Woodruff patted Cassie on the shoulder and bustled out of the room.

When Mrs. Woodruff returned, she was carrying the basket that Cassie always used for her Tuesday deliveries. Cassie held her breath. She must have left the basket in Geoffrey's office. At that moment, she wasn't sure whether she should be relieved not to have left it at Gilbert Grange when she took the dogs. It would certainly have been evidence to back her claim to Sir Edmund.

But having found it in the steward's office was evidence of another kind of transgression: one of the rules of propriety governing unmarried ladies and gentlemen. What must Mrs. Woodruff think of her? And who else knew about it? Cassie imagined her mother's reaction should word get back to the vicarage. She looked anxiously into Mrs. Woodruff's faded blue eyes and found only kindness.

"You'll remember leaving your basket with me on Tuesday so I could give you some of my calves' foot jelly." Mrs. Woodruff set the basket on the table. "I thought you might as well use it for this errand and I'll send the jelly over to the vicarage with one of the stable boys."

Cassie rose from her seat and wrapped her arms around the housekeeper's plump shoulders. "Thank you," she whispered, giving the old woman an extra hug.

"We're that fond of our Mr. Dorton. You just take care of him for us. And see that he receives what he needs," she added, nodding to the basket.

"Oh, my dear Mrs. Woodruff. I do hope I can." Cassie picked up the basket.

The trek from Bradworth Hall to Gilbert Grange seemed endless, but Cassie finally stood before the front door of the Grange, shaking the morning dew off her half-boots, waiting, once again, for someone to answer her knock.

When the door finally opened, the footman's blocky body nearly filled the doorway. If she couldn't get by this man, she would not be able to see anybody.

"I have a parcel I must deliver to Mr. Dorton." Cassie held up her basket.

The footman reached out a meaty hand. "I'll take that."

"No. I must give it to him myself." Cassie kept firm hold of the handle.

"You cannot see the prisoner."

"Mrs. Woodruff gave me special instructions that must be relayed to Mr. Dorton." Gambling that the man couldn't read, Cassie pulled a piece of paper from the basket and handed to him. "Would you care to tell him?"

The footman examined the paper and returned it to Cassie. "I'll ask Sir Edmund."

The moment the footman disappeared through the door, Cassie was up the stairs. She had never been above the first floor at Gilbert Grange, but, after speaking with her father, she had a good idea of where Geoffrey was being held. Hesitating only a moment, she turned right at the top of the second set of stairs and ran down the hall. The door was locked, but the key was still in it. Cassie opened it and slipped in, closing it quietly behind her.

Geoffrey stood with his back to the door, gazing out the window. He was in his shirtsleeves, but Cassie had no time to admire the breadth of his shoulders. "Geoffrey."

"Cassie." Before she had a chance to put the basket down, Geoffrey was across the room. He took the basket from her and dropped it on the chair. Then he took her face in his hands and set his lips to hers. It was the kind of kiss that promised to last a long time, that Cassie would have liked to last forever. It seemed like months since she had last seen Geoffrey, last touched him.

Cassie sank into the kiss, relinquishing all thought, immersing herself in the sensations of Geoffrey's mouth against hers. Like the softest of velvet, his lips whispered over her skin, wiping out any recollection of where she was and what she was about.

"Mmmm." Cassie's hands moved over Geoffrey's broad shoulders, savoring the solidity of his muscles beneath the soft muslin. She slid her hands to his chest and grasped the front of his shirt. Pulling him lower, she returned the kiss for several seconds. Then she flattened her hands against his chest and pulled back.

Regardless of the eternity in the kiss, she knew

where she was and why she was there, and she was certain that Sir Edmund would arrive at any moment. "We must speak quickly."

"How did you get here?" Geoffrey had not released her. He held her away from him and devoured her with his eyes.

"I gulled the footman. Don't distract me." Cassie felt weak in the knees. Fighting the desire to return to Geoffrey's embrace, she backed away from him. "You must tell Sir Edmund I took the dogs." A noise sounded in the hall, and Cassie glanced back over her shoulder.

"You know I cannot do that." Geoffrey dropped his hands from Cassie's shoulders and folded them across his chest.

"We don't have time to argue. Please, please. I cannot bear to think of you imprisoned for something I did."

The door swung open, admitting Sir Edmund and the burly footman. "Miss Hartwell! What do you think you're doing here?"

"Just delivering Mrs. Woodruff's basket." Cassie lifted it from the chair and handed it to Geoffrey, as if to demonstrate her purpose.

"You should not be here. Dorton's got the basket. Now go and hope your mother does not get wind of this . . . this careless behavior." Sir Edmund stepped aside and gestured toward the door.

With a last pleading look at Geoffrey, Cassie turned and left.

Chapter 17

Cassie waited until the last minute and slipped into the back of the Blue Unicorn, hoping to disappear into the crowd. Her mother had forbidden her to attend, but she had no intention of abandoning Geoffrey on this day. She edged toward the heavy curtains shielding the door to the storeroom and scanned the group.

The innkeeper stood at the back of the common room grinning broadly as the citizens of Oakleigh filed in, laughing and talking to each other. They would all be thirsty after the hearing, and he had probably laid in an extra cask of ale just for the occasion. Every face was familiar, and everyone looked pleased about the diversion.

Except for Rodney Gilbert. Rodney sat at the front of the room, arms folded over his narrow chest and his face arranged in its usual sullen scowl. He appeared to be the only person in the room not engaged in animated conversation.

The talk and laughter stopped abruptly, and heads turned toward the door at the back of the room. Sir Edmund stepped into the room, followed by Geoffrey. Geoffrey looked tired and a trifle scruffy, but his clothes were clean and neat, and he held himself with the athletic grace Cassie had grown to love.

Cassie's heart beat wildly as whispered speculation about Geoffrey's guilt filtered through the crowd. This should not be happening. Geoffrey had done nothing to deserve such censure, nothing but protect Cassie's reputation. Cassie stiffened her spine. Come what may, Geoffrey Dorton would not be punished for a theft she had committed.

Once Geoffrey and Sir Edmund had reached the long table set at the far end of the room, the noise subsided and the crowd turned forward, anxious to see what would happen next. Hearings were rare enough in Oakleigh to be a prized form of entertainment. Such a proceeding for a person of some gentility was as good as a play. This had all the earmarks of a day at the fair.

As Geoffrey sat quietly, his eyes scanning the crowd, Sir Edmund read out the charges against him. "How do you answer these?"

"I do not dispute them," Geoffrey said in a quiet voice.

Cassie sidled out of the corner in which she had concealed herself. "Excuse me," she murmured, brushing past several women who had come in too late to find seats. "I must speak—" Cassie stopped dead in the midst of pushing through the crowd at the back of the room.

On the far side, toward the front, sat her mother, dressed in her best blue serge and looking intently toward Sir Edmund. When had she arrived? How could she have gotten into the room without Cassie seeing her? And how could Cassie possibly speak with her mother in attendance?

Cassie shook her head. How could she not speak? It made no difference who was here, she was the only one who could save Geoffrey and there was no question. She must do it. "Your pardon," she murmured to the next person, edging toward the open aisle that would take her to the magistrate.

Suddenly everything in the Blue Unicorn common room came to a standstill. The sound of a heavy carriage was heard on the street, the whispering ceased, and all heads craned toward the front of the building. No one moved or spoke until the innkeeper opened the door to admit two strangers: a man and a woman.

They looked completely out of place in a tiny inn in the middle of Devonshire. At least the woman did. She was tall and graceful and carried herself with an elegance Cassie could only envy. Her luminous skin was set off by dark hair caught up in a heavy plait that was fashioned into a coronet atop her head. She looked like royalty, but there was something familiar about her eyes. Where could Cassie have possibly seen her?

The gentleman was tall and rugged, with tawny hair that had been bleached by the sun and kind lines fanning out from around his extraordinary blue eyes. He looked less regal than the woman, but no less imposing. They were perfect as a couple.

Sir Edmund looked up from his papers, and Cassie's gaze moved in his direction in time to see Geoffrey's startled expression as he rose from his seat. His eyes fixed on the couple, and Cassie could have sworn that a small smile tugged at the corner of his mouth.

"What is going on here?" The stranger's deep voice overwhelmed Sir Edmund's as he strode the length of the room, stopping directly in front of the table.

"And who might you be?" Sir Edmund rose from

his chair, assuming a belligerent posture belied by the slight quaver in his voice.

"I might be Lord Marchbourn," the man said. "And you might be holding my steward without informing me of the fact."

Cassie let out a gasp of relief and sank back against the wall. Thank God. Help had arrived.

"Lord Marchbourn." Sir Edmund dropped back into his seat and immediately popped back up again. "My lord . . . I had no idea . . ."

"You had no idea of what? That this man was my steward?"

Sir Edmund blinked. "Oh no, my lord. I knew that."

"Well, what idea did you not have then? That I wouldn't care if you dragged Lo—Mr.—Dorton before the law without sending word to Marchbourn?"

Although Cassie couldn't see the man's face, something in his tone told her that, despite his sounds of outrage, some part of this situation amused him. Granted, Sir Edmund was frequently ridiculous, but Cassie could find nothing diverting in the possibility of Geoffrey being sent to trial.

"Yes . . . well . . ." Sir Edmund fiddled with the papers in front of him. "I'm sure I meant to. . . ."

"I'm sure you did." Lord Marchbourn's tone was dry as dust.

Sir Edmund looked up in sudden puzzlement. "Why are you here?"

"I have land in this parish. Where else should I be?"

"But if you did not receive a message regarding this hearing . . ."

Cassie felt almost sorry for Sir Edmund. He could not put a foot right.

"Oh, but I did. I just did not receive one from you."

"Uncle!" Rodney Gilbert rose from the bench on which he had been sitting since arriving at the inn.

Sir Edmund glared at him.

"Uncle," Gilbert repeated, "now that Lord Marchbourn is here, I would think that you may proceed with the hearing."

Sir Edmund looked confused.

"No." Lord Marchbourn glanced at Rodney. "He may not. My steward requires legal counsel before you can haul him before a court. I am here to arrange that."

"Very well." Sir Edmund narrowed his eyes at Rodney, who sat back down and folded his arms across his chest.

"And, of course, you will not mind releasing the gentleman into my custody."

Rodney was on his feet again. "Absolutely not. This is not right."

Lord Marchbourn turned his back on Rodney to speak to Sir Edmund. "If there is some doubt as to my trustworthiness, I'm sure I can get someone from St. James's to vouch for me."

Sir Edmund paled. "Oh no. No, indeed. That won't be necessary at all. By all means, take Mr. Dorton."

"And there will be another hearing," Rodney Gilbert said through clenched teeth.

"Uh, yes, of course." Sir Edmund bobbed his head at Lord Marchbourn. "We will send word about another hearing."

"I will send word to you," Lord Marchbourn said, signaling to Geoffrey and marching toward the door where the woman who accompanied him—his wife, Cassie imagined—waited.

Cassie examined Lord Marchbourn's face as he made his way back toward where she stood. It was a kind face and the man seemed to have a care for the welfare of his steward. Her heart fluttered hopefully in her chest. It looked as though Geoffrey was in strong and friendly hands.

When the two men reached the door, Cassie saw the woman reach out as if to embrace Geoffrey. But she stopped, glanced toward the crowd, and dropped her hands, taking Lord Marchbourn's arm instead.

Cassie was unable to tear her gaze from Geoffrey. He had been plucked from this travesty of a hearing by a champion she had summoned. She smiled behind her hands and willed Geoffrey to turn and look at her, to know that she was here. But he did not, too engrossed with Lord and Lady Marchbourn. He left the room without looking at anyone in the crowd. At least he was safe.

Geoffrey and Lord and Lady Marchbourn were not gone a minute before the entire room burst into chatter. Geoffrey Dorton's precipitous delivery from the clutches of the magistrate had proven even more entertaining than the anticipated hearing.

Miss Babson rose from her seat and turned around, scanning the room for someone to talk to. As luck would have it, her regard fell upon Cassie.

"Miss Hartwell, have you ever?" Miss Babson had reached out and grasped Cassie's arm. Her grip was surprisingly strong for one so frail.

Cassie's gaze flashed toward her mother, who was deep in conversation with Mrs. Crocker. Cassie's hope to slip out unnoticed was not served by Miss Babson. She sighed in surrender. "I was glad to see Lord Marchbourn arrive."

"Ooh, he is quite handsome, is he not?" Two little red spots appeared on Miss Babson's cheeks. "Quite imposing and the way he strode up to Sir Edmund. Is it any wonder the squire released Mr. Dorton?"

"Mr. Dorton should not have been here in the first place."

"No, of course not." Miss Babson was as agreeable as always. "I'm sure Mr. Dorton didn't mean any harm by taking the dogs. I know this will all be sorted out in no time now that Lord Marchbourn is here."

"I hope so." Cassie tried to ease her arm out of Miss Babson's grasp.

"Oh, I'm certain of it. Who could gainsay Lord Marchbourn anything he asked?"

Certainly not Miss Babson. Cassie smiled at the old lady. She had probably not had this much fun in years.

Sir Edmund sat at his table, his head down and his face an alarming shade of red. Beside him, Rodney Gilbert stood, tapping his walking stick on the floor in an annoying rhythm and speaking in urgent tones. Cassie could not tell if Sir Edmund's hue was anger or humiliation, but thought that neither boded well for Geoffrey. Cassie wished she were close enough to hear what was being said and, for a moment, considered edging in that direction.

The crowd in the room was not moving, however, and it was impossible to get anywhere until they did. Cassie resigned herself to Miss Babson's effusions.

Fortunately, the innkeeper soon threw open the large side door and began dispensing ale. The crowd moved toward the man with the jug and a lane opened up, allowing those who chose not to indulge to leave by the front door. Mrs. Hartwell finished her conversation and was swept toward the door by the tide of people leaving the tavern.

Cassie patted Miss Babson's hand and, slowly easing her arm away, faded back into the curtains. Her mother was not looking her way. It might still be possible to leave without a confrontation.

Cassie waited until her mother had been gone a full five minutes before she left the Blue Unicorn. Once outside, she leaned against the building, gulping in welcome breaths of fresh air and looking up and down High Street. Her mother was nowhere to be seen, but it would probably be best if she lingered just a few more minutes. And she might learn something of use to Geoffrey if she just waited until the Gilberts left the inn. No one came directly, but soon a familiar figure bumped her right side.

"Brummell." Cassie ran her hand over the big dog's rough head. "Have you been waiting for me?"

Brummell woofed happily and nudged Cassie's hand for more attention.

Cassie ruffled Brummell's ears as she watched the crowd filter out of the Blue Unicorn. The talk was all of the aborted hearing and the conjecture was about Geoffrey's guilt. Cassie felt terrible, and the dog was a comforting presence.

It had been a quarter hour and still Sir Edmund and his nephew had not emerged. Cassie was about to take Brummell and start for home, when she was distracted by a raucous group leaving the Blue Unicorn.

"Did you see t'magistrate's face when Lord Marchbourn walked in?"

"Ha. Likely not to forget it. You'd think he'd never seen no lord before."

"He certainly weren't happy to have the steward snatched out from under him."

"Weren't him was upset. Were the nephew. Did you hear him?"

"Pardon me." Sir Edmund was not three paces behind the group discussing his performance. His tone was icy and his expression rigid.

"My uncle wishes to pass." Rodney was right beside Sir Edmund and not loath to use his walking stick to clear a path. The group broke apart, scattering in several directions and reconvening in front of the livery.

Sir Edmund hurried away, but Rodney stopped for a moment to look around. His glance fell on Cassie and his lip curled. "Did you enjoy the show, Miss Hartwell?"

"I did not come for a show." Cassie was not sure why she even dignified this with a response. She turned to leave. Oh Lord! Her mother was coming out of Mr. Tibbet's shop.

Rodney Gilbert's hand shot out and seized her wrist. She was getting very tired of being grabbed today, but stopped and returned his gaze with a steady stare. "Release my arm."

"When I am ready."

Cassie tried to pull away, and Brummell let out a low growl, circling around to Rodney's left side.

Rodney ignored the dog, maintaining his grip on Cassie. "It appears we have unfinished business."

Cassie yanked against the restraint on her arm. "I have no business with you."

The wolfhound cocked his head toward the man importuning Cassie and lifted his hind leg in the direction of Mr. Gilbert's trousers.

With a yelp, Rodney Gilbert dropped Cassie's arm and leaped to the side. He swung his walking stick in a wide arc, but Brummell was gone, loping down the street with a big, doggy grin on his face.

Chapter 18

Once Lord Marchbourn's carriage was under way, Lady Marchbourn leaned across the seat and hugged her brother. "I am so glad to see you, Geoffrey." She sat back and inspected him. "Although you are looking a bit shabby."

Geoffrey grinned at his fastidious sister. "I have spent the past three days as Sir Edmund's guest. I fear he didn't choose to offer me his finest hospitality. What are you two doing here?"

"Where else would we be?" Lord Marchbourn asked. "We receive a letter from a stranger telling us that Sarah's brother has been incarcerated for stealing dogs, although he did *not* steal the dogs, the letter writer stole the dogs, but no one will believe that she stole the dogs, and we absolutely must get to Devonshire and free *Mr. Dorton*. Mr. Dorton?"

"Cassie wrote?"

"Cassie?" Sarah's astonished look told Geoffrey he would have to answer to his sister for that slip.

"Never mind that now."

Geoffrey smiled at his brother-in-law, grateful for the reprieve. "I thank you, Julian."

"And never mind *that*." Apparently the reprieve was to be short-lived. "I would like you to imagine my surprise when I received this message about my steward, Mr. Dorton. I was quite sure I had sent my wife's brother to Devonshire."

Geoffrey shifted under Julian's gaze. "Well, I could not very well arrive in Devon and say, 'Hello there, I'm the Earl of Cheriton, Lord Marchbourn's new land steward,' could I?"

"I don't know why not. It's not as though this is going to be a permanent position."

"I wanted to be accepted as the steward. No bowing and scraping. No 'yes, my lording.' No exceptions made because I'll be a duke one day. I wanted to make my way here based on my abilities." Geoffrey glanced at his sister during this speech. She would have a much more difficult time understanding his need to prove himself than would Julian.

"And charm the local ladies?" Sarah asked. She had obviously not forgotten about Cassie.

Geoffrey shrugged.

"Tell me about Cassie," Sarah said.

Geoffrey's gaze glanced off his sister's and fell on the window. "We're here," he said, nodding toward the Palladian sandstone building that stood at the apex of the circular drive.

"Oh!" The distraction was successful. Sarah leaned forward and peered up at the building. "It's not as pretty as Marchbourn, but it is quite lovely."

"More imposing." Lord Marchbourn stepped down as soon as the carriage came to a halt and turned to give his hand to his wife.

Geoffrey watched the tender expression on his brother-in-law's face as he helped Sarah from the coach. Yes. When he told Julian and Sarah about Cassie, they would understand.

Tea was served in a small drawing room overlooking the side garden. Mrs. Woodruff had apparently expected the new master and mistress and had everything in readiness. Geoffrey supposed he should not be surprised. He had been without communication for almost four days, and Cassie seemed to have put everything into motion on the first day.

Sarah, at home behind the tea table since she was a girl, distributed cups to Geoffrey and Julian, making sure that the cakes were within easy reach.

"Do you need something more substantial?" she asked, studying Geoffrey.

He waved a hand and then used it to scoop up a large cream cake. "These will do until dinner."

Once Geoffrey had wiped the cream from his fingers and started on his second cup of tea, his sister resumed the attack.

"So," she said, holding up her hand and ticking off items on her fingers. "You have represented yourself as someone you're not, got yourself arrested for stealing, and . . ." She stopped and examined her hand. ". . . compromised a local girl?"

Geoffrey glared at his sister. "I have compromised no one."

"Cassie?" Sarah said. "One does not call a gently bred young lady 'Cassie' unless one is on intimate terms with her. Are you?"

"She is the vicar's daughter, is she not?" Julian asked.

"Yes. Yes, she is." Geoffrey returned to his seat and, leaning forward, took his sister's hands. "But she is much more than that. She is the woman I am going to marry."

"Oh, Geoffrey." Sarah's voice was soft. "Oh my."

Julian set his teacup down with a clatter. "The duke will not be pleased."

Sarah shook her head, and Geoffrey's heart fell.

He well knew that his father was too high in the instep to countenance a marriage between his heir and the youngest daughter of a country vicar. But some part of him had hoped to win the duke's blessing, or at the very worst, present him with a *fait accompli.*

Releasing Sarah's hands, Geoffrey looked at his sister and her husband. They had married with the duke's grudging consent only after Sarah had fled London to be with Julian. His father would be most displeased with another renegade marriage.

"Has Miss Hartwell agreed to this?" Julian's sympathy was evident even though his face was set in a frown.

"I have not asked her yet." Geoffrey examined the bottom of his empty cup. If he were a Gypsy, he might be able to read the outcome there.

"Why not?" Sarah took the cup from his fingers and refilled it, obscuring the future.

"I want to tell her who I am first."

Julian snorted. "Ah yes. Good plan. What girl would turn down a chance to marry a man who had deceived her?"

Geoffrey gazed into his fresh cup of tea. No help was to be found there. "Perhaps it is foolish. But I cannot marry her under false pretenses. She must know who I am and what she will face."

"I dare say you should have considered that when you took on a false identity." Julian was not looking pleased.

"I dare say I should have. But it is too late for that now."

"Do you love her?" Sarah reached out and touched Geoffrey's hand. Trust his lovely sister to ask the critical question.

"I do. And I believe she returns my affection. I believe she loves plain Geoffrey Dorton, land steward, and will be happy to accept Geoffrey Dorrington, Earl of Cheriton."

"I pray you are right."

"Why shouldn't I be right?" Truth be told, he also prayed that he was right. The idea that Cassie Hartwell might not want to marry a future duke was a familiar worry. Geoffrey had wondered about it many times since he laid eyes on the woman he had decided to marry. Was Cassie so different from every other marriageable woman he had ever met? He thought she might be.

Sarah glanced at her husband, who reached out and took her hand.

Geoffrey followed the movement with his eyes and took the lesson it imparted. "If she loves me, she'll not care whether I am a steward or an earl."

Sarah nodded her head. "Quite right. Now we should get her to Bradworth so we may meet her."

Cassie trudged down High Street toward the vicarage, feeling strangely depressed. It was not the encounter with Rodney Gilbert. That had been merely annoying, except for the part where Brummell had lifted his leg and made his opinion known. Cassie smiled. There was a cheering image.

Somehow, she felt let down that Geoffrey had ridden off to Bradworth Hall with Lord and Lady Marchbourn without a word to her—indeed without even a glance in her direction. She supposed she could not blame him. She was, after all, the reason he had been at that hearing. But had she not redeemed herself somewhat by sending for Lord Marchbourn? Or did Geoffrey even know she had done so? Perhaps his employer had chosen not to tell him.

Whatever the reason, she could feel tears building behind her eyes as she approached her home. Unwilling to face her mother in such a state, Cassie wandered past the vicarage and through the gate into the back garden.

Cassie could hear her father's soothing voice issuing from an open window in the back of the house. Latin. The boys must be working on a translation. She crept past the kitchen door and settled herself on the low bench just in back of the apple tree. The sun was low enough to cast deep shadows around the seat. It suited her mood and made her almost invisible.

Drawing her feet up onto the bench, Cassie rested her head against her knees and gazed off into the wooded area that separated the garden from the fields beyond. She rubbed her cheek against the fabric of her gown and remembered Geoffrey's fingers stroking her face. When would she feel that again?

"So there you are." Mrs. Hartwell's voice penetrated Cassie's reverie.

"Here I am, Mama. Is there something you wish?" Cassie straightened, sliding her feet off the bench.

"I wish you would not sneak about in the shadows. Where have you been?" Mrs. Hartwell hurried across the lawn to stand in front of her daughter.

Cassie sighed. She had already lied to her mother about where she was the night the dogs were stolen. She could not bring herself to lie about where she was today. "I was at the Blue Unicorn, Mama."

"I did not see you, young lady. If I had, you may be sure that I would have dragged you out by your ear."

Cassie said nothing.

"Did I not expressly tell you not to attend Mr. Dorton's hearing?" By now, Mrs. Hartwell's hands were fisted on her hips in a posture all too familiar to Cassie.

"I don't believe you did." This was the truth, but the deeper truth was that Cassie knew her mother had not wanted her to be there. And even deeper than that was the truth that wild horses could not have kept her away.

Mrs. Hartwell's eyes closed as if searching for patience. "You know I didn't want you to go."

"Yes, Mama," Cassie said in a subdued voice. "I did know that. But you were there."

"I was there as a concerned member of the community." Mrs. Hartwell blinked once or twice at such a bouncer.

"Yes, Mama."

"But I know very well why you were there, miss."

Cassie met her mother's eyes. She might not agree with her views on many things—including Geoffrey Dorton—but she could not deny that her mother was often acutely perceptive. She did not doubt that her mother knew why she was there and simply waited for the rest of the scold.

"You are much too attached to Mr. Dorton."

Cassie dropped her gaze to her own hands. She had heard this lecture before and would likely hear it again before her future asserted itself.

"I don't know what you're thinking," Mrs. Hartwell continued. "He may be a very nice man and Lord knows he's handsome as you can stare, but he's a steward. You can do much better than a cottage on someone else's estate. Your great-uncle is a viscount." She stopped to take a breath. "And don't roll your eyes at me, missy."

Cassie held up her hand. "Elizabeth," she said, "Susan, Harriet, Martha, Anne, Clara, Eleanor."

"I am well aware of your sisters' names." Mrs. Hartwell's foot began an impatient tapping.

"Every one of them has made a good marriage, Mama. Every one of them is happy, and there is not one title among them." Cassie rose from the bench and would have gone into the house, but her mother put a hand on her arm.

"Then you will be the first," she said.

Chapter 19

Cassie could hardly believe that she and her parents were in the elegant Marchbourn carriage on the way to dinner at Bradworth Hall. The invitation had sent her mother into paroxysms of joy when it arrived, and had been sufficient to pull her father from his study.

"Lord Marchbourn does own this living," Mrs. Hartwell had reminded her husband when he protested that he had a sermon to write. "You would do well to meet him. And this is an opportunity for your youngest daughter to meet the sort of people she should be acquainted with."

And so Mr. Hartwell had put on his best clothes, and Mrs. Hartwell had dressed her hair with extra care. Cassie, at her mother's direction, had pulled out a dress that had been packed in mull muslin for safekeeping and tried, unsuccessfully, to tame her curls. Lord Marchbourn had thoughtfully sent the coach, and the three had bundled in for the short drive.

Mr. Hartwell nodded into a doze as soon as the carriage began to move. Cassie observed him for several moments before turning to her mother. "I thought you did not wish to see Mr. Dorton," Cassie said from the corner of the carriage.

"Don't be ridiculous. The invitation is from Lady Marchbourn. Mr. Dorton will not be there. But I dare say she will have invited Sir Edmund and Mr. Gilbert. And, you know, Lord and Lady Marchbourn may have brought some guests with them."

"They did not come here for a holiday, Mama. They came because Mr. Dorton was arrested."

"Nonsense. They could have sent someone else to deal with such a minor problem. Mark my words, they're here for enjoyment." Mrs. Hartwell's expression bespoke her certainty.

Cassie shrugged and burrowed into the plush velvet seat. She was not about to tell her mother that she thought it was her letter that had brought Lord Marchbourn to Oakleigh.

As the carriage pulled up the drive in front of Bradworth Hall, Cassie's heart began to race. Regardless of her mother's opinion, she could not imagine passing the evening without seeing Geoffrey.

Mrs. Hartwell leaned forward and straightened Cassie's shawl, taking a moment to fluff the tiny sleeves on her best gown. "You look very well, my dear. Pinch your cheeks a bit before we go in. And don't forget to sit up straight."

Cassie examined her sleeves once her mother was finished fluffing. The fine white-on-white muslin was really quite lovely in its simplicity, but Cassie knew that, at the ripe old age of twenty-seven, it was a bit childish for her. As Mrs. Hartwell woke her husband, Cassie pulled the apple-green shawl more closely around her shoulders, hoping it would diminish the impression of a young girl at her first party.

A Marchbourn footman let down the carriage

steps and offered his hand to Mrs. Hartwell. By the time they had all descended to the drive, the imposing front door had been opened, and candle-light reflected onto the columns of the portico.

Lord Marchbourn himself held the door. "Please forgive the informality," he said to Mrs. Hartwell. "We were not expecting to entertain and find ourselves slightly understaffed."

Cassie followed her mother's gaze as she glanced around the entry hall. The marble tile shone and the mirrors sparkled against the damask wall-covering, but it looked decidedly empty. And there was no sound of a party in progress coming from any of the open doors.

"Please do not distress yourself. We are delighted to have been invited." Mrs. Hartwell looked confused, but was all politeness. It was not every day she was invited to dine with a baron's family. Cassie knew that her mother was determined to demonstrate that she was equal to the invitation.

Lord Marchbourn escorted the Hartwells into a small drawing room. Lady Marchbourn, who had been standing in the center of the room, speaking to Mr. Dorton, advanced toward the Hartwells, smiling in welcome. "I am so pleased you could join us for our little family dinner."

Indeed, no one else was present, and Cassie recognized her mother's momentary moue of displeasure. She, however, struggled to suppress her joy on seeing Geoffrey looking groomed, handsome, and at ease.

"Miss Hartwell, you must come sit by me."

Cassie had to tear her eyes away from Geoffrey to acknowledge Lady Marchbourn's request. "Of course. Thank you."

Lord Marchbourn had drawn Mr. and Mrs.

Hartwell into conversation near the fire, and Cassie found herself seated some distance away. Settling onto her seat, she threw a quick glance at Geoffrey, who held himself aloof from both groups. Did he feel ill at ease in the company of his employer?

"I understand you are quite fond of dogs." Lady Marchbourn's amused expression put Cassie instantly at ease.

"Oh my. If only I were not. I am afraid I have mired Mr. Dorton in serious trouble." Cassie glanced at Geoffrey once more and found him looking intently in her direction. She blushed.

"Never mind about that. Julian will set it to rights." Lady Marchbourn patted Cassie's hand. "Do you keep dogs?"

"Dogs?" Cassie dragged her attention away from the man in the corner and back to Lady Marchbourn.

"Yes, do you have dogs of your own?" Lady Marchbourn looked as though she were trying not to smile.

"Forgive me, my lady. I am being unforgivably rude." Cassie was desperate to speak to Geoffrey, to touch him. With enormous effort, she focused her attention on her companion.

Lady Marchbourn reached out and took Cassie's hand, a gesture that startled Cassie into near paralysis. She finally raised her head to Lady Marchbourn and met a gaze of infinite kindness.

"Do you love him?"

It was the last thing Cassie expected to be asked and the last person she expected to ask it. What difference could this possibly make to Lady Marchbourn? Did she take this kind of an interest in the lives of all her employees? Cassie's jaw dropped.

"I am not doing this very well, am I? I am usually

so adept in social situations." Lady Marchbourn glanced over her shoulder at Geoffrey. "I should let Geoffrey explain things, first, I think."

"Oh." Cassie glanced quickly toward her parents. As much as she longed to speak to Geoffrey, she knew her mother would fly into the boughs if she went apart with him. "Oh no. I don't think I should. . . ."

"Dinner is ready, your ladyship." Mrs. Woodruff poked her head in the door. "I beg your pardon for not having it announced more properly."

"Think nothing of it." Lord Marchbourn jumped to his feet and offered his hand to Mrs. Hartwell. "Will you do me the honor?"

Mrs. Hartwell blushed as she put her hand in the baron's and allowed him to help her up. Mr. Hartwell appeared before Lady Marchbourn, and when Cassie rose, she found Geoffrey by her side.

"Miss Hartwell." He held out his arm and she gently laid her hand on it.

Oh, his voice, his touch. Was it only three days ago she had last seen him? Talked to him? Kissed him? Cassie bit her lips to keep from blurting out how glad she was to be with him. Her eyes filled. This would not do.

Afraid to look at Geoffrey, Cassie raised her head and looked toward the door. Lord and Lady Marchbourn had escorted her parents into the dining room. She and Geoffrey were alone. Finally, she turned her gaze to him, drinking in his beloved face.

"Has my sister been filling your ears with tales of my misdeeds?"

"Your sister?"

"Oh Lord." Geoffrey put his hand over hers where it rested on his arm. "Sarah didn't tell you she was my sister."

"Lady Marchbourn said you would explain things. She did not say what those things were. You are her brother?" Cassie experienced a peculiar combination of distress and relief. The knowledge that he was related to Lord Marchbourn's wife seemed at once like a betrayal of her trust and a godsend.

She supposed there was really no need for him to have mentioned his sister. But heavens, it would make it so much easier to convince her mother that she should keep company with Geoffrey.

"Ahem." Lord Marchbourn reappeared in the doorway. "The soup is getting cold."

There was no time to discuss this new information. But Cassie squeezed Geoffrey's arm to let him know that it would be all right, and allowed him to take her into the dining room.

Mrs. Hartwell frowned at Cassie as she took her seat across from her, but her good breeding asserted itself, and Cassie was able to apply herself to the cooling soup without suffering her mother's questions.

Conversation was general and Cassie was charmed by Lord Marchbourn's interest in Devonshire and his knowledge of farming. And now that she knew he was Geoffrey's brother-in-law, she began to understand Geoffrey's interest in the land.

"Lord Marchbourn, do you think you will be able to rectify Mr. Dorton's . . . er . . . problem with Mr. Gilbert?" Mr. Hartwell asked as the first course was removed from the table.

Cassie glanced quickly to her right in time to see Lord Marchbourn's confident smile.

"Oh, I am sure we can come to an accommodation," he said. "After all—"

The diners heard, in rapid succession, a carriage pull up in front of the hall and the echo of the heavy oak front door slamming shut, followed by the rumble of a deep voice conversing with Mrs. Woodruff. By the time the dining room door opened, Lord Marchbourn was on his feet.

"My lord—"

Mrs. Woodruff was cut off by the man behind her. "Never mind that."

"Your grace." Lord Marchbourn looked surprised.

"Marchbourn." The man entered the room and looked around. He was rumpled from travel, but his clothes were of superb quality and fit his broad frame to perfection. He was not tall, but he was impressive. He had a full head of silver hair and eyes that seemed to take in everything at once.

"Sir, to what do we owe the honor of this visit?" Lord Marchbourn signaled Mrs. Woodruff to shut the door and offered his chair to the new arrival.

"Are you going to introduce me?" the man asked, gesturing to the Hartwells, who were all standing by their chairs.

"I beg your pardon. Your grace, may I make known to you Mrs. Hartwell, Mr. Hartwell, and Miss Hartwell? Mr. Hartwell is Vicar of Oakleigh. Ma'am." He turned to Mrs. Hartwell. "His grace, the Duke of Passmore."

"Pleased," the duke said, and took Lord Marchbourn's seat.

Mrs. Hartwell dropped back into her own chair, looking as though she might faint from the honor of meeting a duke.

Cassie was feeling a little light-headed herself. Her gaze traveled around the table. What was going on? Lord Marchbourn had seemed surprised, but not disconcerted. But Geoffrey glowered, first at the duke and then at his sister.

Lady Marchbourn, who had been observing the interaction with a wry smile, picked up her fork and looked up the table. "So, Father, what is this all about?"

Father. It took Cassie several seconds to make sense of what she'd heard. And once it had registered that Lady Marchbourn had called the duke "Father," it took another second or two before she grasped that he must also be Geoffrey's father. She felt every bit of blood draining from her head and thought that she might truly land face-first in the fish. It couldn't get any worse than this.

"That, my girl, is a foolish question. I learn that my only son has been arrested for stealing dogs and you ask me what this is all about?" The duke glared around the table as if he expected someone to deny his right to be there.

His only son? Cassie felt an icy hand grip the back of her neck and feared, for a moment, that she might cast up her accounts. She clutched the edge of the table and took deep breaths, trying very hard to act as though her world had not just been turned upside down.

Chapter 20

Geoffrey paced the floor of the vicarage drawing room. Mrs. Hartwell had greeted him with excessive good will and shown him to the most comfortable chair in the house. But he could not sit. Nor had he been able to sleep. Every time he closed his eyes last night, he saw Cassie's face the moment she had learned he was the only son of the Duke of Passmore. The evening had not gone at all as he had hoped.

His father's arrival in the middle of the first course had led to a hurried meal during which only the most trivial of conversation took place. Although Mrs. Hartwell would have lingered through after-dinner coffee and Lord knew what else, Mr. Hartwell had taken one look at his daughter's ashen face and hurried the family out into the carriage that was to take them home.

Geoffrey was left to face the Duke of Passmore, irate at being dragged from London, at having his only son accused of property theft, and at finding both his son and elder daughter dining with the local vicar and his family. Geoffrey had chosen to put off informing the duke of his marriage plans.

He had retired to the steward's room at the back

of the house, overcoming Sarah's insistence that he sleep in the family wing. All he wanted was the seclusion and comfort of his own place in the house. He was not prepared to be reabsorbed into the Passmore dynasty. He needed time to think and to sleep.

Sleep had not come, so there had been more than enough time for thinking. Unfortunately, little of it was logical. His thoughts teemed with the memories of his every moment with Cassie: his first glimpse of her as he lay on his back in a fallow field, the last time he had held her in his arms, the moment in his office when he realized he loved her.

Why hadn't he told her? If he had spoken of his love then, in the office the night she stole the dogs, if he had told her who he was, if he had asked her to marry him at once, he might be planning his marriage now rather than worrying about whether she would ever speak to him again.

Knocking at the vicarage door had been a trial. Geoffrey had known that Mrs. Hartwell would now be delighted to admit him, and he had no taste for people fawning over his title. However, she was Cassie's mother; meeting her was unavoidable. His only hope was that he could escape from her company without being subject to an excess of toadeating.

Geoffrey stopped his pacing at the front window. It was a brilliant morning, and High Street was alive with people enjoying the morning sun. Geoffrey pictured himself strolling into the center of town with Cassie on his arm. Yes, a walk would be just the thing.

At a sound behind him, Geoffrey turned just in time to see Cassie stumble into the room, her mother at her back. He took a step forward, intending to take Cassie's hand. But, before he reached her, she slid sideways and dropped into the nearest chair. She had not met his eyes.

Mrs. Hartwell bustled forward, looking far too pleased with herself for someone who had just pushed her daughter over the threshold. "Please have a seat, Lord . . . my lord." She gestured toward the armchair in which she had left Geoffrey when she went to fetch Cassie.

Geoffrey waited for Mrs. Hartwell to sit and then complied, his gaze never leaving Cassie's pale face. The bruised look of her eyes led him to suspect she had slept no better than he had. If only she would look at him.

"Here's Dora with the coffee." Mrs. Hartwell gestured to the table by her side, and the little maid of all work did a fair job of setting down the tray and asking her mistress if she would require anything else.

With an effort, Geoffrey transferred his attention to his hostess. "I thank you, Mrs. Hartwell, but I really do not care for refreshment."

Looking flustered, Mrs. Hartwell set the mug she held back on the tray. "Oh. Well, it is very kind of you to call. And we so enjoyed meeting your . . . your family last night."

"Did you indeed?" Geoffrey was certain that, if Mrs. Hartwell had enjoyed the excruciating dinner, she was the only one who had.

"Oh yes. Lady Marchbourn is everything that is charming. So good of her to invite us to dinner. And the duke is so stately. Such a fine figure of a man. It must be quite gratifying to be his son."

Geoffrey shifted in his seat and wished he had been able to see Cassie without dealing with her mother. He had expected the effusions, but they were not welcome.

"And you, my lord. How you tricked us. Why, had we only known who you were . . ." Mrs. Hartwell's voice sank. Doubtless she was recalling how she had treated him when she had not known who he was.

"Actually, Mrs. Hartwell, I have come to ask Miss Hartwell to walk into Oakleigh with me. With your permission, that is." Oh, he was shameless. There was never any question that Mrs. Hartwell would give her permission to do almost anything he wanted to do with her daughter. At that thought, his breathing stopped for a moment, and he could feel the blood rushing to his face. Damn! He had to get himself and Cassie out of here. Now.

"Of course you have my permission, my lord." Mrs. Hartwell beamed at him before turning to her daughter. "Run upstairs and get your bonnet and shawl, my dear. The sun is very bright, but I fear the air may yet be a bit cool."

Geoffrey finally allowed himself to look back at Cassie. She had not risen and, for a moment, he feared that she would gainsay her mother and refuse to walk with him. For several seconds she remained in her seat, looking neither at her mother nor at him. She stared at the floor, her pretty mouth compressed into a grim line. Geoffrey longed to kiss it back into its normal state.

At last, Cassie rose stiffly from her seat and quit the room without a backward glance, leaving Geoffrey to the tender attentions of Mrs. Hartwell, the woman he hoped to be his mother-in-law. If he loved Cassie less, he would have turned tail and run from the room at the first opportunity. He stood his ground and bent what he hoped was a winning smile on the woman.

"I believe I'll have that coffee now, ma'am."

Mrs. Hartwell beamed as she poured the steaming beverage. "Would you care for a muffin?" she asked as she handed the cup to Geoffrey.

He shook his head. "I thank you, no."

"Something else then? Dora will be happy to bring anything you desire."

Geoffrey tried not to cringe visibly. "Please do not go to any trouble. I broke my fast before I left Bradworth Hall."

"Of course." Mrs. Hartwell's eager expression dimmed and she glanced anxiously around the room. "What is taking that girl so long?"

Fortunately, Geoffrey did not have to drink more than two or three sips of the insipid brew before Cassie returned with her bonnet in her hand and her shawl folded over her arm. She stood silently in the door and waited, her face expressionless. Geoffrey had never seen her green eyes look so empty. This was not going to be an easy morning.

At last they escaped the vicarage and Mrs. Hartwell's remonstrations to take all the time they wanted. Cassie had not yet spoken, nor had she even looked at Geoffrey. With every minute that passed, his spirits sank lower.

Geoffrey opened the front gate and, once they had passed through, offered Cassie his arm. Finally, she looked up at him, and Geoffrey's heart stuttered at the message in those huge eyes. Cassie Hartwell was hurt and angry. And he had done this to her. She did not take his arm.

They walked on in awkward silence. Geoffrey had meant to speak the moment they were away from the vicarage, but neither spoke until they were nearly in the center of Oakleigh.

Catching sight of the first shop on High Street, Geoffrey realized that bringing Cassie into Oakleigh would not serve his purpose. Once in town, they were sure to be mobbed by people anxious to learn what had happened since Julian had marched into the Blue Unicorn and snatched Geoffrey from the jaws of justice.

Without asking permission or offering his arm again, Geoffrey grasped Cassie's hand and pulled her through a break in the hedgerow into the very wood in which she'd kissed him on the day of the fair.

The moment they were through the gap, Cassie tore her hand from Geoffrey's and whirled around to face him. Her eyes no longer reflected her pain, but they still glittered with anger. "Just what do you think you're doing, Lord Whatever-your-name-is?"

"My name is Geoffrey." Geoffrey reached for her hands.

Cassie pulled her hands behind her back. "Don't touch me. And you know very well what I mean."

Geoffrey sighed. "Yes. I'm afraid I do. My title is Earl of Cheriton."

Cassie stepped away, turned, and marched deeper into the wood. Geoffrey followed, watching the straight line of her back, reading her mood in the rigidity of her shoulders. She walked until she was below the fateful oak under which they had kissed. Then she stopped and turned to face him.

"Why?" Cassie's voice was a harsh whisper. "Why did you lie to me?"

Geoffrey closed his eyes against the painful acknowledgment of this truth. "I intended to tell you as soon as we had resolved the problem with the dogs."

Cassie's eyes flashed with a parade of emotion. Guilt succeeded anger, to be replaced by sadness. But before she spoke, the fire was back. "Oh Lord. Well, I am sorry about this terrible coil I got you in. But . . . but . . . that does not excuse your own actions."

"No. It does not. There is no excuse for my actions."

"Quite right." Although Cassie nodded for emphasis, something in her voice told Geoffrey that she might relent.

When Geoffrey reached for her hands this time, Cassie let him take them, but when he would have drawn her closer, she held her ground, looking up at him with an odd mixture of determination and confusion. "We have to talk about this, Cassie."

Cassie nodded again and let Geoffrey lead her to an old log on the far side of the oak. He retained one hand as she seated herself and then sat down beside her.

"Why did you not tell me you were the Earl of Cheriton?" Cassie looked out toward the dappled forest floor rather than at Geoffrey.

"I thought I was rather clever, not telling anyone who I was. I was so anxious to be accepted for my work, for myself. You have no idea how dreary it is to have people bowing and scraping to you simply because your father is a duke."

"No. I certainly do not."

Ah. That really said it all, didn't it? The distance he sought to eradicate with his masquerade was even wider now that it was revealed. But he could not let it stand. Geoffrey lifted Cassie's hand and held it between both of his. "You must believe this. I never meant to deceive you."

Cassie jerked her head toward Geoffrey. "No. You meant to deceive everyone. You misunderstand me, Lord Cheriton. I do not feel singled out in any way." Although she did not try to withdraw her hand, Cassie's prim tone served quite well to distance her from Geoffrey.

"That's just the problem, is it not?" Geoffrey

circled Cassie's knuckles with his thumb. "I have singled you out."

"Utter nonsense." Now Cassie did pull away and, straightening her back, sat facing out into the wood with her hands folded tightly on her lap.

"You know it's not nonsense, Cassie. It has not been for quite some time. In fact, I believe it has not been nonsense since the first time I saw you."

Cassie shrugged away from the hand that Geoffrey had placed on her shoulder. "I fear you are deluding yourself, my lord."

"Please, Cassie."

"I think it would be better if you did not use my given name." Cassie's brow contracted.

Geoffrey reached over and ran his thumb down the crease between Cassie's fine, dark brows. "I do not think I can do that, now. Not ever again."

Cassie shook her head. "Please."

"Cassie . . ." Her name came out on a sigh.

Cassie closed her eyes and bit her bottom lip. She shook her head again, but didn't speak.

Geoffrey took her chin between his thumb and forefinger and turned her head toward him. "Please look at me."

Cassie opened her eyes, and Geoffrey almost drowned in the wells of green sorrow.

"I never meant to hurt you, Cassie. I didn't know I would love you."

"Love me? Love me?" Cassie jerked her head from Geoffrey's hand and jumped to her feet. "Love me?" She stood in front of him, hands on her hips, any sadness left in her gaze replaced by a militant scowl.

"Yes. I love you." Geoffrey got to his feet and reached for her. "Will you do me the honor of being my wife?"

"Are you mad?"

This was not the response Geoffrey had hoped for. Nor was it even close to the one he had expected. "I am quite sane, I assure you. But a bit puzzled."

"Are you, indeed? Puzzled because this poor little country girl does not fall into your arms with gratitude at the thought of being a countess?"

"No. Of course not. But I thought . . . I thought you loved me. That night in my office . . ."

Cassie fisted her hands and paced away several steps from Geoffrey. "You mean the night in the steward's office?"

"Yes. That night." Geoffrey's head was spinning.

"I loved Geoffrey Dorton."

Geoffrey's heart leapt, and then he parsed her statement. "*Loved*?"

"Yes, yes, yes. I loved a man who doesn't exist. How do you expect me to feel about that? Grateful that you finally chose to tell me who you were? Grateful to be singled out as the consort of a peer? Grateful to be made an object of curiosity in my town?" Cassie wrenched herself away from Geoffrey and stomped out of the woods.

"Grateful to be loved beyond reason for the rest of your life?" Geoffrey said to the attending trees.

Chapter 21

Cassie heard Geoffrey's voice behind her as she rushed from the woods back to the street, but she didn't stop to listen to what he was saying. Indeed, nothing he said could possibly make her feel better at this moment. She felt like crying, she felt like screaming, she felt like hitting something—preferably Geoffrey Dorton or Dorrington or Lord Cheriton, or whoever he was. The man she thought she loved.

Right now, anger was the emotion in play, and although she could not scream, Cassie kicked at the loose stones in the road, scuffing her second-best pair of half-boots and startling a flock of sparrows out of the hawthorn bushes. Above the sudden rustling of leaves and rush of wings, Cassie heard another sound. Geoffrey had followed her. Lengthening her stride, Cassie tried to leave him behind.

"Miss Hartwell . . . Cassie . . ."

No. She would not stop for him. Would not speak to him. She stopped and turned. "Go back to London, Lord Cheriton. You are quite out of place here."

"I cannot. I cannot leave you like this." Geoffrey hesitated for only a moment, then was at her side.

"How would you like to leave me, then? In a pud-

dle of tears by the side of the road? Waiting at my
window for a glimpse of you as you ride past on
your return to town? Pining for your return in the
certain hope that I will one day be a duchess?"

"Cassie, I—"

Cassie held up her hand. "There is nothing you
can say that would make this right."

"May I call on you again?"

Cassie sighed. The bewilderment in Geoffrey's eyes
reached her in a way his words had not. But what was
she to do? She shook her head. "I don't know."

Geoffrey reached out to touch her face, but Cassie edged away, continuing to shake her head. She
looked at Geoffrey for a long moment, trying to
read what was in his eyes, in his heart. But her own
heart was in too much turmoil to make any sense of
Geoffrey's. So she left him, turning away and biting
her lips to hold back the tears until she reached
sanctuary.

The duke was the last person Geoffrey wanted to
see when he returned to Bradworth. In fact, Geoffrey would have been happy to see no one for the
next several years. He turned his horse over to a
groom, went straight to the steward's office, and
buried himself in his ledgers.

The lines of figures marched down the page, but
all Geoffrey could see was Cassie's solemn face. The
room was quiet except for the sound of workers
moving across the courtyard, and yet he could hear
Cassie's voice, accusing him of deceit and worse.
He pushed back from the desk, giving up any pre-
tense of work. He could concentrate on nothing
but Cassie's pain and his own.

It was true. He had deceived her. Indeed, he had

deceived everyone in Oakleigh, but none of them had received the blow Cassie had. Geoffrey called himself every kind of fool. He had deceived the woman he loved. Now he was paying the price. How was he to convince her that he loved her still? He dropped his head into his hands and closed his eyes. There she was, green eyes ablaze with anger, lips tight with pain. Oh Lord! Even if she was persuaded of his love, the real problem was making her realize that she loved him in return.

Geoffrey had not been back more than fifteen minutes when a servant knocked on the door to tell him he was wanted in the house, a servant who called him "my lord" and who had actually backed out of the room after delivering the message. Geoffrey swore under his breath. Reluctantly rising from his chair, he followed the footman out of the room.

"You wanted to see me, your grace?" Geoffrey was relieved to note that his interview would not be strictly private. Sarah and Julian were both in the drawing room and were both looking quite sympathetic. And well they should, having been confronted with the duke's displeasure themselves on one or two occasions.

"Tell me about the hounds."

"Sir?"

"You did not steal those dogs, Cheriton. Of that I am absolutely certain." The duke stood near the fireplace, fingering his watch fob and examining Geoffrey with the basilisk stare he generally reserved for recalcitrant members of parliament and impertinent tradesmen.

"Why, thank you, Father. I am gratified by your confidence in my character." Out of the corner of his eye, Geoffrey saw Sarah wince.

The duke's cold stare dropped several degrees.

"Do not be insolent, boy. I demand to know how you came to be in possession of allegedly stolen hounds, and how you came to be arrested for their theft. The question of why you are masquerading as a commoner will be left for a later conversation."

Geoffrey scanned the room. He was aware that Cassie had told his sister and her husband that she had taken the dogs, and he was pleased that they were protecting his Cassie.

"I am waiting for an answer." The duke's quiet voice demanded attention.

"I regret that I cannot give you one." Geoffrey glanced at his sister, who gave him an encouraging smile.

"I will not be gainsaid, young man. I am your father and I have the right to know what caused this debacle."

"Father, believe me. I would tell you were I at liberty to do so." Geoffrey took a step toward his father and looked him in the eye. "But I cannot."

"Whom are you protecting?" The duke glared around the room, seeking an answer from anyone who would provide one.

"I have nothing more to say on this subject." Geoffrey stood his ground in front of the duke, who refused to drop his gaze.

"What do you expect me to do, then?"

"I expect nothing, your grace. I feel sure that Julian and Sarah will assist me in my problem."

"Hmph!" The duke drew back his shoulders and left his position by the mantel to walk to the window. "Nice park, Marchbourn."

"Thank you, your grace." Julian glanced quizzically at his wife. She gave her head a minute shake, and Julian said no more.

The duke spent several more minutes examining

the landscape outside the window. "You could do with a few more gardeners," he said finally.

"Hmmm." Julian nodded at his father-in-law's back. Geoffrey stared at them both, waiting for the duke to get on with whatever was on his mind.

"You're m'son, the next Duke of Passmore," the duke said after a few more minutes staring out the window.

Geoffrey nodded. This went without saying.

"I certainly don't intend to leave my heir languishing in jail. We'll go to the magistrate and resolve this problem first. Then we will deal with the reasons for it."

"We?" It took a supreme effort for Geoffrey not to goggle at his father.

The duke nodded, but turned his attention to Julian. "You had better come as well, Marchbourn. You're the landowner here."

Julian looked nearly as surprised as Geoffrey felt, but left his position to stand beside Geoffrey.

The duke looked back out the window. "It's a fine afternoon. We shall ride to this Sir . . . ?"

"Edmund," Geoffrey said. "Edmund Gilbert."

"Sir Edmund's home. And you can show me what you've done with the land."

"What Geoffrey has done," Julian said. "I arrived just before you did."

Without looking around, the duke grunted.

Geoffrey flinched. At this particular moment, it would have been better not to remind his father that he had been parading around Oakleigh disguised as a land steward.

It was a fine afternoon, and Geoffrey almost enjoyed the ride across the Bradworth fields toward

Gilbert Grange. The planting was nearly complete and everything looked in good order. The riders stopped at the top of a small rise, and Geoffrey followed Julian's gaze as he took in the evenly plowed rows in one field and the activity in the neighboring one.

Julian grinned at Geoffrey. "My compliments. The land is in excellent condition, thanks to you."

Feeling absurdly gratified, Geoffrey prayed that the heat in his face was due to the effects of the mid-afternoon sun in the nearly cloudless sky. At least there was this one thing he had done properly since he arrived in Devonshire.

No one spoke for the rest of the ride, an occurrence that gave Geoffrey even more time to dwell on his problems. Every thought led back to Cassie. How would she react to Julian's praise of his work at Bradworth? What would it mean to her if his father convinced Rodney Gilbert and Sir Edmund to drop their charges? Had he crossed the line to the point where she would never speak to him again? Could she love him enough to forgive him? What might he do to persuade her to marry him?

The sound of the horses' shoes against the paved surface of the Gilbert Grange courtyard pulled him out of his reverie.

"Still with us, are you, Geoffrey?" Julian pulled up beside him.

The duke had already dismounted and was waiting for a groom to come and take his horse. Geoffrey and Julian joined him on the cobbles, and Julian stepped up to knock on the door. But before he could lift the knocker, the door opened, revealing Sir Edmund's butler.

"Your grace." The man bowed and backed away

from the door, sweeping them in with an expansive gesture.

"My, word certainly travels quickly here," Julian murmured to Geoffrey as they followed the duke into the dim reception hall.

"If you will walk this way." The butler marched off toward the stairs as if leading a parade. Geoffrey saw his father roll his eyes, but they all followed.

Sir Edmund and Rodney were both in the formal sitting room, both dressed in pristine linen and freshly brushed coats. Geoffrey glanced at his brother-in-law. Word certainly did travel fast.

"Your grace, Lord Marchbourn." If it were possible to bow lower than his butler, Sir Edmund achieved it.

Geoffrey glanced at Rodney Gilbert out of the corner of his eye. He looked as though he did not know which way to turn. The younger man obviously wanted to make an impression on someone as lofty as the duke. It was equally obvious that it still rankled to show any deference to Geoffrey.

"You of course know my son, Lord Cheriton." The duke gestured toward Geoffrey as if Sir Edmund could not possibly have thought he was a land steward mere days ago.

Sir Edmund blanched, but managed another bow toward Geoffrey.

Trying not to smirk, Geoffrey used the regal nod that always worked for his father. "Your grace, allow me to make known to you Sir Edmund Gilbert and his nephew Mr. Rodney Gilbert. Sir Edmund, my father, the Duke of Passmore, my brother, Baron Marchbourn."

Sir Edmund bowed once more to the duke. "My nephew is often in town. Perhaps you have seen him there."

The duke pulled a quizzing glass out of his waistcoat and turned it on Rodney Gilbert. After a lengthy inspection, he turned back to Sir Edmund. "I have not."

Rodney turned an ugly shade of red, and Sir Edmund looked longingly toward the decanters standing on the sideboard. "Ah—er—yes. Pray be seated. May I offer you a drink?"

"No. We won't be long." The duke took a seat, indicating to Julian and Geoffrey which ones they were to assume.

"Of course, your grace. I can guess what brings you here." Rodney Gilbert shifted on his feet, and Sir Edmund shot a minatory look at his nephew before continuing. "I can assure you that, had we known who Mr. Dorton, that is, Lord Cheriton, was, we would never have subjected him to . . . ah . . . to . . ."

"To abject humiliation?" Julian suggested.

The duke cleared his throat, and Julian fell silent. "Now that you know who he is, however . . ."

"Indeed, now that we know who he is, we certainly have no intention of making him stand trial." Sir Edmund glanced uneasily at his nephew.

"Excellent." The duke prepared to stand. "Well, that was quite expeditious. We shall leave you."

"Ah, well . . ." Sir Edmund looked as though he was about to swallow his tongue. "The fact is—"

"The fact is that my hounds were taken and were found at Bradworth Hall." Rodney Gilbert's color was still high, but he had assumed a placating smile as he leaned confidingly toward the duke.

"Quite so." Julian looked at his father-in-law and then at Geoffrey before continuing. "Then, of course, some restitution must be made. Without an imputation of guilt, of course."

"Of course." Sir Edmund nodded.

"I want to buy the pack." Geoffrey spoke for the first time since he had made the introductions.

"What?" Julian's eyebrows shot up.

"I want the hounds. I offered Mr. Gilbert an excellent price for them earlier. I offer him one hundred pounds now."

Gilbert sprang from his chair to face Geoffrey. "One hundred pounds? You offered more than that."

"So I did. But you declined that offer. Now I'm offering you one hundred pounds. Far more than the pack is worth."

"Why do you want them? Do you hunt?" Gilbert's brows drew together in a suspicious frown.

"I merely want them. Think of it as a prerogative of rank." Geoffrey felt quite proud of his affectation of hauteur. His father couldn't have done it better. He wondered if the duke had started out this way or if he had been born with the ability. He polished off the performance with a nonchalant inspection of his fingernails.

"Of course, my lord." Sir Edmund had risen to stand beside his nephew, doing a passable impression of bowing and scraping. "No one here would question your desire for such a fine pack of hounds. I'll have my stable master deliver them to Bradworth Hall, shall I?"

"That would be acceptable," Geoffrey said, getting out of his chair and moving toward the door. "Are you coming, Father?"

Chapter 22

"You have done what?" Cassie shot to her feet. She had just shut the door to her bedchamber and thrown herself onto her bed, when her mother came in, glowing with excitement over her news.

"I have invited the Bradworth party for dinner. It is only proper to return Lady Marchbourn's kind invitation."

"The entire party?" Cassie dropped back onto the bed, picked up her pillow, and clutched it to her breast.

"Of course, of course. This is an ideal opportunity for us, my dear. It is obvious that Lord Cheriton has tender feelings for you. Why, if you do as I say, you could be a countess before Christmas." Mrs. Hartwell looked around the room. "What are you doing here? I thought you had gone for a walk."

"My walk is over, and I came in here to be alone for a while." Cassie waited, hoping her mother would leave. She really did not want to talk about dinner with Geoffrey and his family and she most assuredly did not want to talk about what went on during her walk.

Mrs. Hartwell plucked the pillow from Cassie's grasp, plumped it into shape, and placed it back on the bed. "Lord Cheriton probably had to attend his father—the duke," she said with a complacence that left Cassie biting her tongue rather than refute her.

"Doubtless," Cassie said.

"I'm sure he'll return tomorrow. Lord Cheriton has been smitten ever since he laid eyes on you. How well I remember." Mrs. Hartwell smiled happily at a memory Cassie knew to be totally false.

"I'm sure you do, Mama. You went out of your way to discourage him that first day he saw me home. And several times thereafter."

"Oh, that does not signify. Lord Cheriton is used to the ways of elegant ladies. He will know that I was only protecting my daughter's reputation."

"Oh, Mama. He is not going to marry me. I wish you would not have him to the vicarage." Cassie thought she might scream if her mother said "Lord Cheriton" one more time.

"Too late for that now, missy. I sent an invitation this morning while you were out walking with your beau."

Cassie left the bed and paced around the room, trying her best not to glare at her mother. "Not my beau. Not my suitor. I'm not even sure he likes me at this point. Can you not see how uncomfortable it will be for all of us if the Bradworth party comes for dinner?"

"Pure rubbish. Lady Marchbourn is all that is kind, and I'm sure we will find the duke to be equally charming once we become better acquainted. After all, if he is to be your father-in-law . . ." Mrs. Hartwell smoothed the coverlet and walked to the door. "Are you coming?"

"I think I'd rather remain here, Mama." Cassie looked back toward the bed. Was there any way to prevent her mother from her foolish machinations? Matchmaking with a duke's son would only embarrass Cassie and the rest of the family.

Mrs. Hartwell shook her head and was about to leave, when Cassie stopped her. "When is this dinner?"

"Tomorrow."

"Has Lady Marchbourn accepted, then?" Cassie rubbed her hands along her arms, seeking a warmth that wouldn't come. She could not remember ever feeling so alone in the midst of her family.

"Not yet. But I assure you, she will." Mrs. Hartwell hurried out with the same enthusiasm with which she had entered, and Cassie threw herself back onto the newly straightened bed.

As her mother's footsteps receded into the distance, Cassie rolled onto her back, once again clutching the pillow. She could not remember feeling as confused as she felt right now. She had treated Geoffrey very badly this morning. She had berated him and refused to listen to his explanation. But what explanation could possibly suffice considering the magnitude of his deception?

Groaning, Cassie rolled onto her side and stared out the window. How could the weather be so beautiful when she was so miserable? Geoffrey's deception. That rankled. But her own response to it bothered her even more. Why should she be so angry about a silly masquerade? It was not as if he had made any promises to her. It was not as if the fact that he would one day be a duke made any difference in how they were with each other.

Except . . . except for those kisses and more than kisses. Except for the night she had brought him the hounds and he had held her in his arms and, without words, seemed to promise a future together.

No! Cassie sat up and flung her pillow to the side.

No. She would not read promises where none were made. He had kissed her. But she had kissed him, as well, had she not? These were the actions of two people who found each other pleasing. She had been kissed before Geoffrey. Why should his kisses mean any more than those others?

But he asked you to marry him, a voice whispered in her mind. Groaning, Cassie sat up and put her head in her hands. So he had. He had said he loved her. Said he wanted to marry her. And she had thrown it back in his face. Was she a fool? Perhaps, for treating Geoffrey so. His deception, painful as it was, had not been wicked. Nor had it been meant to injure. And she loved him, so she would forgive him—probably.

But marry him? Enter the *ton* at the highest levels? One day be a duchess? Even her brave spirit quailed at the thought. Nor could she believe his father would allow it.

Very well, she would attend her mother's dinner—as if she had any choice—and she would treat Lord Cheriton as the brother of Lady Marchbourn and someone she might see from time to time when his sister was in residence in Devonshire. Or she might not. Oh, bother. Cassie could not even tell which would be worse.

"Dinner at the vicarage?" The duke looked aghast.

"Yes, Father. We have received a very handsome invitation from Mrs. Hartwell, and it is only right that we go." Sarah folded the invitation and tucked it into her book.

"Utter nonsense. I have four estates in the country and have never felt it necessary to dine with the clergy. Send the vicar a nice donation for a new church roof and be done with it."

Geoffrey stood in the corner of the room, listening to his father and sister debate the invitation that had arrived while he was out walking with Cassie. His heart was pounding so hard he thought it must be audible to everyone in the room. He had not been this nervous since he was eleven and had to confess to his father that he had finished off an entire decanter of his best port. It was time to tell the duke that he wanted to marry the vicar's daughter, and he knew his father would be seriously displeased.

"Father." Geoffrey stepped out from the corner to stand before the duke. "It is important to me that you accept the invitation."

"Important to *you?*"

"Yes." Geoffrey hesitated a moment, trying to regain control of his breathing. "Yes. I would like you to know Miss Hartwell, as I intend to marry her."

"Marry her?" The duke rose from his chair in a fluid motion and stood toe to toe with his son, glaring.

"Yes, sir."

"Is this some sort of puerile joke, like trotting off to Devonshire and working the land under an assumed name?" The fact that he was inches shorter than Geoffrey did not make the duke any less intimidating.

"Neither of these things is a joke. Both are important to me. But nothing is as important as Cassie Hartwell."

The duke turned to his daughter and son-in-law. "Do you hear this? This is all your doing. Letting him go off to be a steward, of all things. Now he has been ensorcelled by some conniving female."

Julian made no response, and Sarah stared at her father with her guileless hazel eyes. Geoffrey could almost read her mind. His sister was a woman who understood the sacrifices love sometimes required.

"Bah! I should know better than to appeal to you." The duke returned to his seat, glowering at the room in general.

"I want you to meet her, Father." Geoffrey had not moved during the duke's small tantrum.

"I did meet her, young man. She was that mousy thing at table the night I arrived, was she not? Never opened her mouth, as I recall."

"No. That was not Cassie."

"I beg your pardon. Has this vicar more than one daughter with her talons in you?"

Geoffrey bit his lips. He had never before felt the urge to strike his father. "First of all," he said, his voice icy, "Cassie Hartwell does not have her talons in me. In fact, I have a rough road ahead if I am to convince her to marry me."

The duke snorted.

Geoffrey held up his hand. "Secondly, the woman at the table was in no fit state to be met due to your precipitous interruption of our meal. No. You have yet to meet the woman who is to be your daughter."

"Hear me well, Cheriton. No vicar's daughter will be the future Duchess of Passmore if I have anything to say about it."

"You have nothing to say about it, your grace. The only duchess you may choose is your own." Geoffrey took the seat opposite his father and folded his arms across his chest.

"Father." Sarah's gentle voice floated into the conversation.

The duke's gaze slid away from Geoffrey toward his daughter. Geoffrey tracked the movement, recognizing the stubborn cant to his father's jaw. This would not be a concession easily won.

"I know you want the best for us. I remember how hard it was for you to accept my marriage." Sarah reached out and touched her husband's arm. "But we are no longer children. You must trust us to know what is in our interest."

Scowling at both his children, the duke shook his head. "I have nothing against Marchbourn," he said to his daughter. "From all I can see, he's turned out to be a good husband, and he knows his duty to the crown. But you could have been at the highest levels of London society instead of mired in the wilds of Somerset. You could have made a difference."

Sarah's mouth formed a stubborn line, and she raised her chin to glare at her father. "I do make a difference."

The duke waved her objection away. "It all makes no difference now. You're Marchbourn's wife and that's all there is to be said about it. But it's not too late for your brother to make the appropriate marriage for his position."

Geoffrey leaned forward. "The appropriate marriage is to a woman of my own choosing. I will not be married for dynastic purposes, no matter what you think is right."

"Nonsense. I'm not talking about a dynasty. Any good breeder with a decent pedigree will do for that."

Geoffrey shivered at the image conjured by his father's words. "Then what is your point?"

"When I'm gone, you'll be the Duke of Passmore. It's a title with some honor and responsibility. You will need a wife who is able to meet your peers as an equal, who will not shame you in society, and whose family name will augment your connections."

Geoffrey hesitated. "I understand your position, your grace, but I do not necessarily enter into your sentiments. Miss Hartwell is a lady, the equal of anyone she might meet in town. There is nothing about her that would shame me."

"But who is her family? Her father is a country vicar. And her encroaching mother, where is she from?" The duke folded his arms across his chest.

"Mrs. Hartwell is the daughter of a gentleman, the niece of a viscount, if that is what will satisfy you."

"It does not satisfy me." The duke shook his head. "But I will attend this dinner with the vicar."

"And you will not sabotage Geoffrey's suit?" Sarah asked.

"I reserve judgment about the suit," the duke said, his jaw clenched in a belligerent grimace. "But I assure you, I know how to be courteous to my inferiors."

Geoffrey sighed.

Cassie was afraid to put her wine-glass to her lips. The tension in the room was so pronounced that she feared she would bite right through her mother's crystal. She gazed at her plate, gripping her fork so hard it bit into her fingers.

The moment the party from Bradworth Hall had walked in the front door, Cassie knew the evening would be dreadful. Her mother had given new meaning to sycophancy. Every time she spoke to the duke, Cassie could see the man's jaw clench. And to make matters worse, she was sure this was all very amusing to Geoffrey. How glad he must be that she had not taken him seriously.

But Geoffrey did not seem to be laughing at her. Whenever Cassie looked up, she found his solemn gaze upon her. She didn't know what to think, and determined not to look at him at all. This, however, turned out to be almost impossible. When Cassie was not looking at her plate or staring into the wine-glass she didn't dare drink from, her gaze was drawn to Geoffrey, seated to her right in an obvious ploy by her mother.

Cassie watched her father struggle valiantly to keep the conversation afloat.

"Have you read Epictetus's *Discourses*?" he asked his guests.

Cassie could almost see the duke's eyes rolling back in his head. Lord, could this be any worse?

"Do you not care for your wine, Miss Hartwell?"

Cassie started at the sound of Geoffrey's voice so close to her ear, nearly spilling some of the claret in the process. "Ah, not at this moment." Cassie hastily replaced her glass. "Are you well, Lord Cheriton?" Lord, what a pitiful excuse for conversation. Yet, she could never say what was in her head and in her heart.

"Tolerably so." Geoffrey picked up his own wine-glass.

"Mr. Gilbert has not been unreasonable?" A shimmer of distress passed through Cassie.

"No. Not at all. The matter has been resolved."

"I am relieved to hear it." Cassie relaxed enough to take a sip of her wine.

"Are you talking about the dogs?" Julian asked from across the table.

Geoffrey glanced at his father. "I was telling Miss Hartwell that the matter has been resolved."

The duke looked up from his poached partridge. "Still don't know what you're going to do with a pack of hounds."

Geoffrey shook his head, but the duke kept talking.

"If you don't want them, I suppose I could have them sent up to Dorrington Hall. They're not first rate, but I dare say the master of the hounds up there could find something to do with them."

"You bought the hounds?" Cassie felt a little pang in the region of her heart. Geoffrey had rescued the dogs.

Geoffrey waved a hand. "Gilbert has no need for them and I wanted some return for my money."

Cassie flushed. She was not fooled. Geoffrey had done this for her. But what was she to do with this knowledge? She wanted to reach under the table and grab his hand in gratitude. Or she wanted to flee the room and go upstairs for a good cry. She wanted to be with Geoffrey and she wanted to tell him to take his good deeds back to London.

The meal was concluded in tolerable civility. But Cassie's confusion was so great that she found it impossible to meet Geoffrey's eyes until the last of the fruit was removed. Gratefully, she followed her mother and Lady Marchbourn into the drawing room.

When the gentlemen joined them for coffee, Cassie was startled to find the duke seating himself next to her.

"Miss Hartwell."

"Your grace." Cassie refused to be intimidated. This was likely the last time she would ever speak to the Duke of Passmore. She had nothing at stake.

The duke removed his quizzing glass from his waistcoat and examined her through it.

"Do you find that useful?" Cassie asked.

Startled, the duke dropped the glass. "I beg your pardon?"

"Do you see who I am more clearly with that?"

Cassie gestured toward the glass, now dangling on its chain.

The duke retrieved the article and put it back in his pocket. "Are you mocking my vision?"

"Oh no. It never occurred to me that you couldn't see me. Can you not?" Cassie wondered if she had just blundered very badly.

The duke sat back and studied Cassie in earnest.

Cassie was unable to interpret the strange look that came over his face. "Pray forgive me, your grace. I really did not mean to offend."

"Hmmph. Take more than that to offend me, young lady." The duke leaned forward. "Tell me about the hounds."

Cassie's face heated. "I stole them. And I brought them to Bradworth for safekeeping."

The duke nodded. "Plain speaking. Good girl. Did my son know you were going to take them?"

"Oh my heavens. No. It was an impulse. Perhaps a foolish one. I saw Mr. Gilbert beating them and I couldn't leave them in his care."

"Can't abide a man who beats his animals. Never could."

"No, your grace. Nor can I."

The duke's lips twitched in what Cassie thought might be a smile. "Perhaps I don't need that glass to see you," he said.

Cassie relaxed a bit, smiling at the duke. Despite his austerity, there was something about him that reminded her of Geoffrey. Perhaps it was the eyes. Now a faded blue, they must have once been the dancing blue of his son's. Would Geoffrey look like the duke when their children were grown? Cassie's breathing faltered. What was she thinking? She and Geoffrey would never have children. Her heart wept.

"Your pardon." Suddenly, Geoffrey was standing

before Cassie and his father. "Lady Marchbourn wishes to depart soon, and I hoped Miss Hartwell would show me the garden before we left."

Cassie glanced at the duke, but could read nothing in his impassive expression.

"Go on, girl. We can't have him looming over us like this. Most . . . uncomfortable." The duke stared up at his son, and Cassie saw a small frown of— what—disapproval?

Although Cassie stood and took Geoffrey's arm, she did not allow him to take her to the door. "We cannot walk out alone together."

Geoffrey cocked an eyebrow at her, but turned and spoke to his sister.

Lady Marchbourn left her seat immediately and moved to stand beside Cassie. "I would dearly love to see your herb garden, Miss Hartwell."

The moon was new, and there was barely enough light to see the old apple tree, let alone the herb garden. But Cassie allowed herself to be swept out of the house by Geoffrey and his sister.

No sooner had the back door closed behind them than Lady Marchbourn took Cassie's hand and squeezed it. "I would be very happy if you were my sister," she said before melting into the darkness, leaving Cassie alone with Geoffrey.

Cassie listened to Lady Marchbourn's footsteps recede into the darkness. Although her eyes had not yet adjusted to the dim light, she could feel Geoffrey's presence beside her with every inch of her skin. She could smell him: clean linen, fresh air, leather. She thought she would be able to recognize him in thirty years by that scent.

Geoffrey moved closer and took Cassie's hand. Cassie knew that she should speak, move away, return to the house, but she could not bring herself to do any of these things. All she knew was that it felt so good to be this close to Geoffrey, so comfortable to have his calloused hand enclosing hers. All she remembered was that he had bought Rodney Gilbert's dogs, and it was a gift to her.

Without thinking further, Cassie turned so that she was directly in front of Geoffrey. She reached for his other hand and, pulling him closer, stood on tiptoe and searched for his mouth with hers.

Geoffrey groaned and leaned down to meet her, his lips covering hers with an unexpected urgency. Releasing her hands, he gathered her to him and kissed her with the fervor she remembered from their embraces in his office.

Allowing doubt to fade away, Cassie slid her arms around his waist and kissed him back. This moment was for her, for them. Cassie stepped outside of time, with no thought to what had brought them here and no promises of tomorrow. She drank in the warmth and tenderness of Geoffrey's kiss and refused to think about the next moment.

Chapter 23

"Miss Cassie! Miss Cassie! You must come."

Cassie looked up from her book. She had spent the morning on the bench under the apple tree, trying to forget the previous evening. The meal had been painful enough, but saying good-bye to Geoffrey before he had climbed into the carriage with a baron and a duke had been far worse. The gulf between them had never been wider than the one created by the crest on the carriage door.

Would it have been better if Geoffrey had not kissed her? Or rather, if she had not kissed him? As sweet as the memory was, the kiss was still a painful reminder of what she could not have. And it was over too soon, broken by Lady Marchbourn's low voice telling Geoffrey that they must leave.

Cassie shook her head, trying to dislodge the memory. "What is it, Robert?"

Reverend Hartwell's three students skidded to a stop in front of her. "Farmer Jenkins's dog is hurt and he's going to shoot him dead."

"Brummell?" Cassie swung around to face the boys.

"Yes, miss. The big wolfhound."

"Where is he? What's wrong with him?"

"He's at the farm. Can't tell what's wrong. Looks as though he's been beaten bad. He's all bloody, and he might have a broken leg."

"Mr. Jenkins says he can't use a dog with only three legs," one of the younger boys interrupted.

"You shouldn't have left him." Cassie rose and started toward the gate.

"Mr. Jenkins said he wouldn't do anything 'til you got there," Robert said, trotting along at her side. "We made him promise."

Cassie stopped in the road and looked around. She would need a way to transport the injured dog. "Where is my father's dog-cart?" she asked the boys.

"Vicar took it to make calls, Miss Cassie. Mrs. Brown's ailing and he said he had to see her."

Something had to be done quickly. She would need to bring the dog home to nurse him. "Run to Bradworth," she said to the oldest boy, "and tell whoever you can find that we need a cart at Mr. Jenkins's farm. I'll see to Brummell."

Without looking back, Cassie hurried across the field, her mind fixed on her friend, Brummell. "No, no, no." The words slipped from Cassie's lips with every step. She could not imagine anyone wanting to hurt the dog. He was a friend to everyone in Oakleigh. The next moment, she recalled the big dog expressing his displeasure with Rodney Gilbert by lifting his leg against the man's trousers.

Cassie shook her head. Now was not the time to wonder who had done this, nor to assign blame. All she wanted right now was to get to poor Brummell.

The moment Cassie climbed over the last stile onto Mr. Jenkins's farm, she saw the big dog lying by himself on a pile of straw in the shade of a thatched outbuilding. Cassie's heart plummeted; he was not moving. Farmer Jenkins was nowhere in sight, and Cassie wondered if he'd already shot the poor beast.

Then Brummell raised his head and looked at her. His tail gave one feeble thump, and he dropped his head back onto the straw. Cassie picked up her skirts and ran. Dropping to her knees beside Brummell, Cassie stroked his great head. The dog heaved a huge sigh and tried to lick her hand.

"Oh, Brummell." As she soothed the dog, Cassie looked at the dried blood that had stiffened patches of his rough gray coat and at the awkward angle of his left hind leg. "Who did this to you?"

"Don't know."

Cassie started. "Mr. Jenkins. You surprised me."

"Poor beast came limping home at dawn looking like this." The farmer waved a hand at Brummell, who replied with another thump of his tail.

"The boys told me you planned to shoot him." Cassie looked up at the farmer from her position beside Brummell, shading her eyes with her hand to block out the bright morning sun.

Mr. Jenkins shook his head. "He's no good to me with three legs," he said, repeating what the boys had told Cassie.

"I hope you'll forgive me for asking, Mr. Jenkins. But what did he do for you with four legs? He really seems to spend most of his time wandering."

"Oh, aye. He's a social one, that dog. Out all day, gadding about the neighborhood, making friends with everyone he sees. But, at night, there's none better at keeping the foxes away." The farmer looked down at the dog. "Or there was. I reckon he won't be much use with a game leg."

"You mustn't shoot him." Cassie's hand came down gently on Brummell's neck. "I'll take him

home and nurse him. And if he cannot use that leg,
I'll keep him."

"You sure the vicar won't object? He eats as much
as two men." The farmer looked skeptically at the
big animal.

"I assure you, my father would not want to see
such a gallant animal killed."

The farmer sighed. "Take him then. But I have
no means for you to move him."

"The boys are to come with a cart."

"Got it all planned out, have you? Well, he's yours,
but I have work needs doing. I'll leave you to it." Mr.
Jenkins tugged at his forelock and moved off.

"Thank you, Mr. Jenkins. I promise I'll take good
care of him."

"Indeed, miss. I know you will." The farmer returned to his chores and Cassie leaned back over
Brummell, trying to assess the extent of his other
injuries.

Slowly, Cassie ran her hands over Brummell's body,
stopping to calm the dog whenever she found a particularly tender spot. Brummell lay patiently and allowed his friend to examine him, raising his head
when she located an injury and, only once, growling
softly when she came too near his injured leg.

He had been badly beaten. He had bled in several places, and the leg was definitely broken.
Cassie could not tell if that was the only broken
bone. She dared not examine the dog too closely.

Brummell's head flopped back to his straw bed,
his breathing changing into a shallow pant. He no
longer seemed to know Cassie was there.

"Oh no." Cassie tried to rouse him, but he lay, un-
responsive, beneath her hands. "Don't die," she whispered, laying her head on the straw near the dog.

Brummell grunted, and Cassie sat up to look at

him, tears running down her cheeks. "Brummell," she whispered, smoothing the fur around the dog's ears. "You're still with us."

"We'll take care of him, my love." Strong hands cupped Cassie's shoulders.

"Geoffrey." Cassie turned to find Geoffrey kneeling beside her. "I didn't hear you come."

"Of course not. You have something more important engaging your attention."

For a moment, Cassie allowed herself to lean against Geoffrey's broad chest, allowed his arms to come around her, allowed him to press his lips to the top of her head.

"Can you help?" she asked.

Geoffrey reached out and stroked Brummell's muzzle. "He looks very bad."

"Oh, Geoffrey. Poor Brummell. Who would do this—never mind. I'm just so worried that he will die." Realizing she was gripping Geoffrey's buckskin-clad thigh with one hand, Cassie released it, her face flooding with color.

Geoffrey squeezed her shoulder, responding only to her concern for the dog. "I've brought the cart, but I'll need help moving him."

Swiftly, Cassie rose to her feet and disappeared into the barn, returning after a short while with Farmer Jenkins and a rather battered-looking door.

"Oh, excellent notion, Miss Hartwell." Geoffrey placed the door next to the unconscious dog and signaled the farmer to move to the other side. "On my count, Mr. Jenkins, we'll slide him onto the door and then carry it to the cart. Are you ready?"

With much shifting and some little effort, the makeshift litter was loaded onto the cart. Geoffrey shook Farmer Jenkins's hand, lifted Cassie up onto the seat of the cart, and then climbed up himself.

As he guided the cart out of the farmyard, Geoffrey glanced over at Cassie. Her green eyes were mirrors of worry in her pallid face. Geoffrey's heart lurched. She loved the injured wolfhound. And when Cassie Hartwell loved, she loved with her whole being. Right now, everything she had was concentrated on the poor beast in the back of the cart. But Geoffrey knew that she would give herself to him just as completely once she decided to love him.

"We'll go slowly so as not to jostle Brummell too badly." Geoffrey reined the pony to the right as they drove through the farm gate.

"Where are you going? Oakleigh is that way." Cassie pointed to the left.

"To Bradworth. George Kingsley knows more about doctoring animals than we will ever learn."

"I can't ask you to do this." Cassie's brow creased into a worried frown. "If Brummell is at Bradworth, I cannot see him every day."

"Why ever not?" It occurred to Geoffrey that Cassie's desire to see the dog daily would throw her into his path as well and would be very much to his advantage. He suppressed a smile.

"Well . . ." Cassie flushed. "I cannot inconvenience Lord and Lady Marchbourn."

"Think nothing of it. My sister will be delighted to further your acquaintance."

"Yes, but—"

"But it makes more sense for Brummell to be where George can look after him. You know this." Geoffrey turned in his seat and looked at Cassie. "What is really bothering you?"

Cassie didn't answer. Instead, she twisted around

on the bench to look back at Brummell. "He's still breathing."

"He will be all right, Cassie. You'll see." Geoffrey prayed that he was right. The dog meant a great deal to Cassie, and Cassie meant even more to him.

The rest of the trip to Bradworth Hall was accomplished in silence. It was a short distance, but Geoffrey had sufficient time to gauge the mood of his companion. Her concern was palpable, as was the underlying current of unease that Geoffrey feared was due to his proximity. With every turn of the wheels, he longed to take her in his arms and offer the solace she needed.

Cassie alternated between looking back to make sure that Brummell still breathed and casting surreptitious glances in Geoffrey's direction. She had been worried enough about the dog to send to Bradworth for a cart. Surely she must have suspected that such a request would also bring Geoffrey. Geoffrey hoped that some hidden part of Cassie's heart had known that he would come, had wanted him to be with her.

Out of the corner of his eye, Geoffrey watched Cassie fidget on the cart bench. This was not the time to broach what was in his heart, although every moment he was with her seemed fraught with hidden meaning.

Cassie turned once and looked directly at him, her eyes asking the questions he longed to answer. Then she straightened her shoulders and turned her attention to the road ahead. Her moods had been mercurial since learning of his title. Geoffrey prayed she had forgiven him his deceit, but he felt the constraint that still existed between them. His job now was to remove whatever obstacles to their future remained in Cassie's mind.

Geoffrey was not surprised to find a large party gathered in the Bradworth stable yard, awaiting their arrival. George Kingsley and Lord Marchbourn took charge of Brummell's litter, while Geoffrey swung Cassie down from her seat and set her directly in front of Lady Marchbourn.

"Come along, my dear. You look like you could use some tea." Lady Marchbourn put an arm around Cassie's shoulders.

"I thank you. But I really must be with Brummell." Cassie looked pleadingly at the woman.

Lady Marchbourn smiled sympathetically. "Of course. Once he is settled, make Geoffrey bring you to the house."

Cassie nodded noncommittally and hurried off after the men.

By the time Cassie reached the stall the stable master had arranged for Brummell, Geoffrey and Kingsley had begun to splint the animal's leg.

"There you are," Geoffrey called as she approached. "Come and soothe your dog. He's beginning to wake and this is going to hurt like the very devil."

Cassie slipped into the stall and sat down on the clean horse blanket that had been laid out for the dog. Taking Brummell's head into her lap, she stroked his nose and murmured words of comfort.

With great care, the stable master finished splinting Brummell's leg. After a good deal of whining and yipping, the dog flopped back onto his blanket in patent relief. George Kingsley fetched a bucket of water and clean rags and began to swab the dried blood and debris from the wolfhound's other injuries.

"Will he be all right?" Cassie asked, trying to keep

Brummell from jerking as the men worked on the worst of his wounds.

"Can't say." Kingsley looked up from his task. "He's a good strong dog, and if we can keep the wounds from infection, I think he'll live. Won't know about the leg for a bit."

Finally, it was over, and the big dog lay exhausted on his blanket. Geoffrey did not stand as Kingsley left the stall, but looked up with a smile of gratitude. "Thank you, George."

"I'll have the boys keep an eye on him. And I'll check him regular," the man said. "Now, don't you worry."

After Kingsley left, Geoffrey eased a little closer to Cassie and put an arm around her shoulders. Intent on the dog, she did not pull away, relaxing a little into his embrace.

"Come into the house for some refreshment. Sarah will be expecting you."

Cassie shook her head. "I'd like to stay awhile with Brummell. Then I must go home."

Geoffrey considered trying to talk Cassie into staying at the hall, but knew that right now Brummell was her concern. And, because he loved her, Brummell was also his. "We shall do whatever you desire, my love." He tightened his arm and felt Cassie's momentary resistance give way. She folded into him and let him hold her. Geoffrey smiled into her hair. At least she allowed him to offer comfort. It was a start.

Chapter 24

"Let me help you with that." Mrs. Hartwell took the brush from Cassie's hand and deftly arranged her mass of curls into an artful froth. An accomplished lady's maid could not have done better.

"What is this, Mama? Are you thinking of going into service?"

"You have a caller, missy, and I don't want you dawdling over your hair."

"Lord Cheriton?" Cassie peered up at her mother's reflection in the mirror. Of course it was Geoffrey. No one else would prompt her mother to take up the fine art of dressing hair.

Mrs. Hartwell nodded, reaching out to pluck free a few curls around Cassie's face. Her cat-in-the-cream-pot smile told Cassie all she needed to know about her mother's state of mind.

"Is it Brummell?"

"Brummell? It's Lord Cheriton." Mrs. Hartwell's smile was replaced by a look of confused concern that made Cassie bite her lips to keep from chuckling.

"Oh, never mind." Cassie glanced at the mirror before leaving her dressing table. Her hair really looked quite nice. She hugged her mother in passing and ran out of the room.

Geoffrey stood at the foot of the stairs looking unpardonably handsome. Nearly tripping as she hurried down to him, Cassie called, "Is he well?"

Geoffrey turned toward her, a crooked smile on his lips. "Your dog is making a remarkable recovery, Miss Hartwell. I have come to take you to him."

"You have?" Cassie's heart performed a complex somersault. Damn Geoffrey Dorrington for being kind and considerate as well as handsome. How was she ever to come to terms with losing him if he persisted in such perverse behavior?

Geoffrey offered his arm and opened the front door, revealing a gleaming curricle standing in the lane.

"Oh, Lord Cheriton." Mrs. Hartwell had come up behind them. "How very elegant. Is that yours?" She nudged Cassie with her elbow. Cassie ignored her.

"No, ma'am. I have borrowed it from Lord Marchbourn."

"Oh, well, I dare say you have an even better one of your own in London."

"In fact, I haven't. I spend most of my time in the country, where one of these things is most impractical."

"In the country?" Mrs. Hartwell looked as though she could hardly believe her ears. "But you must go to court, attend balls and . . . and routs."

"I am a farmer, Mrs. Hartwell." By now, Geoffrey had released Cassie's arm and was facing her mother.

Cassie had rarely seen her mother look more confused. "Well, you had us fooled into thinking so," Mrs. Hartwell said, after considering this statement for a moment.

"You misunderstand me, Mrs. Hartwell. I am still

the Earl of Cheriton. But the earl is a man who is interested in farming."

Cassie could tell that this explanation did little to enlighten or comfort her mother. But when Lord Cheriton took Mrs. Hartwell's hand and, bowing over it, said, "I promise to take excellent care of your daughter," her mother's frown was placed by a bright, complacent smile.

"I shall have her home in time for supper," Geoffrey added.

"Oh, take as long as you want, my lord. I know I can trust you with my dearest child. I am certain you have only her best interests at heart."

"Mama," Cassie murmured, mortified.

But Geoffrey beamed back at Mrs. Hartwell. "I assure you, I do, ma'am."

Out in the lane, Geoffrey whisked Cassie off the ground and deposited her in the curricle. He had not yet donned his gloves, and the warmth of his hands through the thin cotton of her gown sent a frisson of awareness through Cassie's body, causing her face to heat and her toes to curl. She chided herself for foolishness and set about smoothing out the wrinkles in her skirt as she waited for Geoffrey to join her on the seat.

Geoffrey rounded the curricle and climbed up. Before picking up the ribbons, he reached under the seat and pulled out a pair of very fine driving gloves.

As he began to pull on the left glove, Cassie noticed that his knuckles were raw and, in one or two places, bleeding. She put her hand on his arm to stop him. "What happened?"

Geoffrey hesitated and looked down at his hands. "Nothing," he said, continuing to work his hand into the glove.

"Nonsense. What have you done to your hands?"

Cassie pulled the glove away from Geoffrey and took his right hand into both of hers. She looked from the hand to his warm, blue eyes. "Have you been fighting?"

Geoffrey shrugged. "No. Not fighting. I had an errand to take care of and thought to dispatch it this morning before I called for you."

Cassie searched Geoffrey's face. There were no marks anywhere but his hands, but the hands had definitely been in a fight. "Are you hurt?"

"I am not hurt," Geoffrey said, freeing his hand and lightly touching Cassie's cheek before pulling on his gloves and reaching for the reins.

As Geoffrey moved the horse out into the lane, Cassie turned her attention to the day, trying to distract herself from the lingering sensation of Geoffrey's fingers against her face. The morning sun, reflected off the dusty lane, only increased the warmth caused by Geoffrey's nearness, by the tenderness of his touch.

But it was obvious to Cassie that those very hands had been put to a more martial purpose before he came to fetch her. Geoffrey had been fighting, but had not sustained any blows. That much was obvious from his unmarked face and pristine jacket.

"Have you seen Mr. Gilbert?" Cassie asked, taking her eyes from the road to examine Geoffrey's profile.

He grimaced. "Now that you mention it, I did see him earlier."

Cassie said nothing and they continued toward Bradworth in silence.

Slowing to drive through Oakleigh center, Geoffrey spoke again. "But I dare say we won't be seeing much of him in the future."

"Indeed?"

Geoffrey nodded.

"He's the magistrate's nephew," Cassie said, worry springing to life inside her.

"He's a bully." Geoffrey snapped the reins as they left the town, urging his horse into a trot. "And he has discovered urgent business in town."

As they approached the gates to Bradworth Hall, Geoffrey turned toward Cassie. "Will you walk with me after we call on Brummell?"

Cassie's heart set up a clatter. Her feelings had been at war with her common sense ever since she learned Geoffrey's true identity. There was no doubt that he was still the man with whom she had fallen in love. But there was also no doubt that he and his family were so far above her touch as to make an alliance between them laughable. And the thought of being a duchess frightened her down to her toes. What did Geoffrey want to say to her? What did she want him to say? She had no answer and so gave none.

"You say Brummell is doing well?" Cassie asked as she and Geoffrey entered the stable. She was answered by a basso woof from the far end of the block.

"As you hear." Geoffrey smiled as he ushered her toward the dog's hospital stall.

Brummell was sitting up, his splinted leg out to one side and a jaunty bandage around a shoulder. When Cassie rounded the corner into the stall, he woofed again and then sighed, his tongue lolling out in happy greeting.

Cassie dropped to her knees in front of the big dog, and was rewarded with a great, sloppy lick to her cheek. Rubbing her face on her sleeve, she turned to Geoffrey. "Did you give him fish?"

Geoffrey grinned and passed her his handkerchief.

"He looks grand. Thank you. Thank you." Cassie smiled up into Geoffrey's eyes.

"Thank George Kingsley. And your friend Brummell. He has a heart the size of Devonshire." Geoffrey reached down and patted the dog, snatching his hand away before Brummell could lick it.

Cassie spent a few more minutes talking to the wolfhound and examining his bandages. When she was done, she looked up at Geoffrey, feeling suddenly shy. "I think he has no need of me today," she said, raising her hand.

Geoffrey helped Cassie to her feet. Tucking her hand in the crook of his arm, he said, "Then it is time for our walk."

Cassie looked at the crumpled handkerchief still in her other hand. "Perhaps I might wash up?"

"Hmmm." Geoffrey gave an exaggerated sniff. "Yes, perhaps you should."

"Oh!" Cassie's mood lightened at Geoffrey's teasing. She was smiling when Geoffrey opened the door to the Bradworth Hall kitchen and stuck his head in, calling for water and towels.

Once Cassie had washed off the evidence of Brummell's affection, she and Geoffrey left the hall's back garden for a stroll through the large park that sloped gently from the back of the estate. Geoffrey led the way past a walled garden that had been too long neglected and through the flowering border to an avenue of elms, overgrown with encroaching ground plants. It was dark and cool and secluded.

At the end of the avenue, a small bridge spanned a stream and ended in an even more secluded grotto, furnished with a stone bench that had recently been brushed clean and upon which reposed a very comfortable-looking cushion. Cassie glanced at Geoffrey. This had been planned.

After seating Cassie on the cushion, Geoffrey stood in front of her, looking down at her in silence. Cassie's heart beat a rapid tattoo. She knew what was coming and had no idea how she would respond.

Geoffrey dropped to one knee and took her hand. Cassie blushed furiously, shaking her head in supplication. "Please," she said.

"I must say this." Geoffrey held her hand between both of his.

Cassie heaved a huge sigh. "Then sit beside me and say it."

Without relinquishing his hold on her hand, Geoffrey did as she requested. "Miss Hartwell—my Cassie—will you do me the honor of becoming my wife?"

Cassie sighed again, her eyes filling. "I appreciate the honor you do me in asking." She stopped and examined Geoffrey's dear face.

"Yes?"

"I am sorry, my lord, but I cannot marry you." The words came out in a rush, and Cassie attempted to release her hand from Geoffrey's grasp.

"Call me by my name," Geoffrey said, refusing to let go of Cassie's hand.

"Don't you see?" Cassie said. "It makes no difference what I call you, you are still Lord Cheriton and I am still the vicar's daughter."

"Is that the problem?" Geoffrey looked stunned.

"Of course that's the problem. What did you think?"

"Do you love me?" Geoffrey tugged at Cassie's hand and shifted closer to her.

Cassie had to tilt her head to meet Geoffrey's eyes.

"Do you?" Geoffrey's voice was urgent.

Cassie dropped her gaze. "That is not the point."

"That is the only point." Geoffrey placed a knuckle beneath Cassie's chin and lifted her head so that she would look at him. Then, in a whisper of movement, he touched his lips to hers. "The only point," he murmured against her lips when the kiss had ended.

For a moment, Cassie clung to Geoffrey, wishing that things might be different, that there was some way to cross the great gulf their births had created between them. She dropped her head to his shoulder and sighed.

"What is it?" Geoffrey cradled her in one arm, using the other to stroke back the hair from her forehead.

"I cannot be your wife, Geoffrey. The woman you marry will, one day, be a duchess."

"Do you not want to be a duchess?"

Cassie raised her head, a trickle of amusement threading through her at the incredulity in Geoffrey's voice. "No. I do not."

"Do you want to be my wife?" The quiet hope in this statement extinguished Cassie's amusement and forced her to face her own desires.

"I do, Geoffrey. I love you and I can think of no greater joy than to be your wife, but . . ."

"But you will not make the sacrifice."

Sacrifice? Cassie pulled back, taken by surprise at this statement. "I am not the one who would make the sacrifice."

"Who then?" Geoffrey took her shoulders in his hands and forced her to look directly at him.

"You. Your father. Your family. If you marry me, my connections will be a degradation to you." There. It was out. He could have no answer for that.

"What nonsense. Do you love me?"

"I have said I do. And I do more than I can say."

"Come with me." Geoffrey leapt to his feet and grabbed Cassie's hand, pulling her up after him.

"Where are you taking me?" Cassie scrabbled

for her bonnet as Geoffrey tugged her away from the bench.

"To prove a point."

Cassie had to run to keep up with Geoffrey's long strides. In half the time it had taken them to find the grotto, they were back at Bradworth Hall and through the French windows that led from the back garden into the family drawing room. Lord and Lady Marchbourn were in quiet conversation in one corner of the room, and the Duke of Passmore was at a desk, engaged in correspondence. They all looked up as Geoffrey flung the door open and dragged Cassie into the room.

"Father."

As Cassie stood panting at Geoffrey's side, the duke laid his quill on the desk and cocked his head at the two of them. "Yes?"

"Did you love my mother?"

"I beg your pardon." The furrow between the duke's brows deepened. Cassie could see he was as confused as she was, and not at all pleased with the question.

Geoffrey grasped Cassie's hand when she tried to sidle away. "This is important, Father. Miss Hartwell must hear your answer."

The duke turned his frown on Cassie. "Must she indeed? To what end, may I ask?"

Lady Marchbourn glanced at Geoffrey's face and turned toward the duke. "Father . . ."

The older man glowered, first at his daughter and then at Geoffrey. He held this expression for what seemed a very long time before relenting. "Very well then. I loved your mother very much, Geoffrey, as I am sure you are aware."

"Do you like being a duke?"

"Geoffrey . . ." The duke drew out the name into a long growl, beginning to rise from his chair.

"Do you?"

"I am passably good at it," the duke said.

"You are more than good," Lady Marchbourn said from her seat in the corner. "You know very well that the government would be in dire trouble without you."

The duke shrugged, but Geoffrey took up the refrain.

"You know Sarah is right. All of London knows it."

Cassie glanced up at Geoffrey as he spoke. She did not know it, but she had no reason not to believe that the Duke of Passmore wielded considerable power. He certainly looked like a man of authority. But what had this to do with her?

"Do you like being a duke?" Geoffrey asked again.

"It's who I am." The duke's expression had softened, but he still did not look pleased with this inquisition.

"Indeed," Geoffrey said softly and, looking down at Cassie with a tender gleam in his eye, added, "And it's who I will be one day."

"As I have been telling you." The older man picked up his quizzing glass and began to play with it.

"Well?" Geoffrey squeezed Cassie's hand. When she looked up again, he smiled at her briefly and then returned his attention to his father.

"Yes. Damn it. I like being a duke. Now what is this all about?"

"Should you have liked being a duke with a wife you didn't love?" Geoffrey looked intently at his father as he delivered his final thrust.

"Ah." The duke collapsed back into his seat, his face a study in dawning realization. "I see." He looked down at his correspondence, then back up at Geoffrey before continuing. "No. No, I should not."

"Would you have me be the next Duke of Passmore with a wife I did not love?" Geoffrey persisted.

The duke sighed. "No, son. I would not."

"There." Geoffrey turned to Cassie. "You see? I cannot be a good duke without you."

Cassie's heart skittered. In a single conversation, Geoffrey had disposed of the major obstacle to her happiness. "But I don't know how to be a duchess." The words came out in an embarrassing squeak.

Geoffrey took both her hands in his. "My dearest girl. No one knows how to do a thing when they begin. We will learn together."

From behind her, Cassie could hear Lady Marchbourn's soft voice. "Just say yes."

Geoffrey looked down at her, his eyes so full of love that Cassie was flooded with warmth. How could marrying someone who looked at her like that ever be a sacrifice?

"Just say yes," he whispered.

So she did. And then, in front of the Duke of Passmore and, for all Cassie knew, the rest of the world, Geoffrey Dorrington took her in his arms and kissed her well and thoroughly. And she kissed him back, forgetting where they were, who was there, forgetting everything but the knowledge that she was safe in the arms of the man she loved.

When the kiss ended, Cassie glanced around the room and then looked up at Geoffrey. Warmed by the love in his smiling blue eyes, she repeated her promise. "Yes. Yes, I will marry you."

More Regency Romance
From Zebra

__A Daring Courtship   0-8217-7483-2 $4.99US/$6.99CAN
  by Valerie King

__A Proper Mistress   0-8217-7410-7 $4.99US/$6.99CAN
  by Shannon Donnelly

__A Viscount for Christmas 0-8217-7552-9 $4.99US/$6.99CAN
  by Catherine Blair

__Lady Caraway's Cloak   0-8217-7554-5 $4.99US/$6.99CAN
  by Hayley Ann Solomon

__Lord Sandhurst's Surprise 0-8217-7524-3 $4.99US/$6.99CAN
  by Maria Greene

__Mr. Jeffries and the Jilt 0-8217-7477-8 $4.99US/$6.99CAN
  by Joy Reed

__My Darling Coquette   0-8217-7484-0 $4.99US/$6.99CAN
  by Valerie King

__The Artful Miss Irvine   0-8217-7460-3 $4.99US/$6.99CAN
  by Jennifer Malin

__The Reluctant Rake   0-8217-7567-7 $4.99US/$6.99CAN
  by Jeanne Savery

Available Wherever Books Are Sold!

Visit our website at www.kensingtonbooks.com.

More Historical Romance From
Jo Ann Ferguson

__A Christmas Bride	0-8217-6760-7	**$4.99US/$6.99CAN**
__His Lady Midnight	0-8217-6863-8	**$4.99US/$6.99CAN**
__A Guardian's Angel	0-8217-7174-4	**$4.99US/$6.99CAN**
__His Unexpected Bride	0-8217-7175-2	**$4.99US/$6.99CAN**
__A Rather Necessary End	0-8217-7176-0	**$4.99US/$6.99CAN**
__Grave Intentions	0-8217-7520-0	**$4.99US/$6.99CAN**
__Faire Game	0-8217-7521-9	**$4.99US/$6.99CAN**
__A Sister's Quest	0-8217-6788-7	**$5.50US/$7.50CAN**
__Moonlight on Water	0-8217-7310-0	**$5.99US/$7.99CAN**

Available Wherever Books Are Sold!

Visit our website at www.kensingtonbooks.com.

Discover the Romances of
Hannah Howell

My Valiant Knight	0-8217-5186-7	**$5.50US/$7.00CAN**
Only for You	0-8217-5943-4	**$5.99US/$7.50CAN**
A Taste of Fire	0-8217-7133-7	**$5.99US/$7.50CAN**
A Stockingful of Joy	0-8217-6754-2	**$5.99US/$7.50CAN**
Highland Destiny	0-8217-5921-3	**$5.99US/$7.50CAN**
Highland Honor	0-8217-6095-5	**$5.99US/$7.50CAN**
Highland Promise	0-8217-6254-0	**$5.99US/$7.50CAN**
Highland Vow	0-8217-6614-7	**$5.99US/$7.50CAN**
Highland Knight	0-8217-6817-4	**$5.99US/$7.50CAN**
Highland Hearts	0-8217-6925-1	**$5.99US/$7.50CAN**
Highland Bride	0-8217-7397-6	**$6.50US/$8.99CAN**
Highland Angel	0-8217-7426-3	**$6.50US/$8.99CAN**
Highland Groom	0-8217-7427-1	**$6.50US/$8.99CAN**
Highland Warrior	0-8217-7428-X	**$6.50US/$8.99CAN**
Reckless	0-8217-6917-0	**$6.50US/$8.99CAN**

Available Wherever Books Are Sold!

Visit our website at **www.kensingtonbooks.com**

Embrace the Romance of
Shannon Drake

When We Touch
0-8217-7547-2 $6.99US/$9.99CAN

The Lion in Glory
0-8217-7287-2 $6.99US/$9.99CAN

Knight Triumphant
0-8217-6928-6 $6.99US/$9.99CAN

Seize the Dawn
0-8217-6773-9 $6.99US/$8.99CAN

Come the Morning
0-8217-6471-3 $6.99US/$8.99CAN

Conquer the Night
0-8217-6639-2 $6.99US/$8.99CAN

The King's Pleasure
0-8217-5857-8 $6.50US/$8.00CAN

Available Wherever Books Are Sold!

Visit our website at **www.kensingtonbooks.com**.

Celebrate Romance With One of Today's Hottest Authors

Amanda Scott

__**Border Fire**
0-8217-6586-8 $5.99US/$7.99CAN

__**Border Storm**
0-8217-6762-3 $5.99US/$7.99CAN

__**Dangerous Lady**
0-8217-6113-7 $5.99US/$7.50CAN

__**Highland Fling**
0-8217-5816-0 $5.99US/$7.50CAN

__**Highland Spirits**
0-8217-6343-1 $5.99US/$7.99CAN

__**Highland Treasure**
0-8217-5860-8 $5.99US/$7.50CAN

Available Wherever Books Are Sold!

Visit our website at **www.kensingtonbooks.com**.